MUDDY BANKS

This is a Chaparral Book

MUDDY BANKS

by RUBY C. TOLLIVER

Illustrations by WALLE CONOLY

TEXAS CHRISTIAN UNIVERSITY PRESS
FORT WORTH

NINTH PRINTING

Library of Congress Cataloging-in-Publication Data
Tolliver, Ruby C.
Muddy banks.

Summary: A twelve-year-old runaway slave is torn between desire for freedom and affection for the woman who has protected him, as the impending Battle of Sabine Pass threatens to engulf their part of Texas.

1. Sabine Pass, Battle of, 1863—Juvenile fiction. 2. United States—History—Civil War, 1861–1865—Campaigns—Juvenile fiction. [1. Sabine Pass, Battle of, 1863—Fiction. 2. United States—History—Civil War, 1861–1865—Campaigns—Fiction. 3. Texas—History—Civil War, 1861–1865—Fiction]
I. Title.

PZ7.T5748Mu 1986   [Fic]   85-20851
ISBN 0-87565-062-7
ISBN 0-87565-049-X

Design by Whitehead & Whitehead
Illustrations by Walle Conoly

THIS BOOK IS PRINTED ON AND BOUND WITH ACID-FREE MATERIAL.

Also by Ruby C. Tolliver:

Decision at Sea
Summer of Decision
More than One Decision
Decision at Brushy Creek
A Question of Doors

Other Chaparral Books available:

Duster by Frank Roderus
Letters to Oma, A Young German Girl's Account of Her First Year in Texas, 1847, by Marj Gurasich
Lone Hunter and the Cheyennes by Donald Worcester
Lone Hunter's Gray Pony by Donald Worcester
Luke and the Van Zandt County War by Judy Alter
Stay Put, Robbie McAmis by Frances Tunbo
Tame the Wild Stallion by Jeanne Williams
The Last Innocent Summer by Zinita Fowler
War Pony by David Worcester

*For Josie Patrick, who believed,
and for Grace Allred,
who first made it possible.*

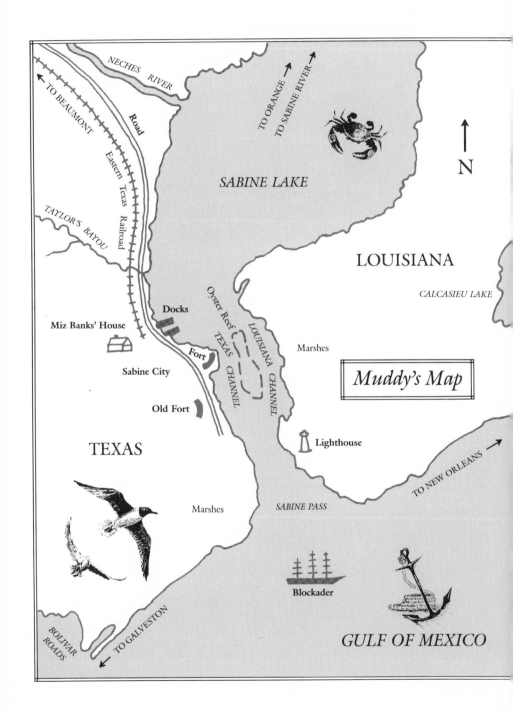

NECHES RIVER

TO BEAUMONT

Road

Eastern Texas Railroad

TAYLOR'S BAYOU

TO ORANGE

TO SABINE RIVER

SABINE LAKE

N

LOUISIANA

CALCASIEU LAKE

Oyster Reef

LOUISIANA

TEXAS CHANNEL

LOUISIANA CHANNEL

Docks

Miz Banks' House

Fort

Marshes

Muddy's Map

Sabine City

Old Fort

Lighthouse

TEXAS

Marshes

SABINE PASS

TO NEW ORLEANS

Blockader

GULF OF MEXICO

TO GALVESTON

BOLIVAR ROADS

Prologue

THE STATE OF TEXAS refused to recognize Lincoln's Emancipation Proclamation issued in January of 1863. Until that year, Texas saw little Union military action in the Civil War. But Lincoln was determined to sweep Texas back into the Union fold. The Federal forces wanted Texas' plentiful stores of beef and corn, and the bulging warehouses of cotton bales were needed to make ammunition.

When the Confederate military sensed the imminent invasion of Texas, over eleven thousand troops were routed to the "Arkansas station" on the Red River to defend against an anticipated assault on Shreveport, Louisiana, and the probable conquering of Texas. Although Texas had sent seventy thousand troops to the Confederacy, few if any defenses were maintained along the Texas shoreline on the Gulf of Mexico.

Our story, set on that shoreline, begins in March of 1863.

Chapter 1

NOW! IT HAD TO BE NOW! Boy squeezed
his black skinny body between the cotton bales tied to the gun-
mount on the starboard side of the Confederate steamer. He gasped,
but clenched his jaws tight, silencing the rising cry of pain. He must
not cry out loud. The man on lookout might hear. Twisting with all
his might, he could see a jagged cut on the calf of his leg. His dirty
cotton trousers had offered no protection, and he had not noticed
the rusty point of the ship's anchor protruding between the two
bales of cotton. Fear of discovery numbed the stinging pain. The
blood on the cotton did not sicken him. He had seen blood before,
and he knew what he must do.

He pressed his wound hard against the rough, tightly pulled
burlap cover of the nearest bale. A few tense moments passed and
the trickling fingers of blood halted in their downward reach. Now
he must leave. He dared not wait any longer.

Barely discernible in the twilight of early dawn, the ship's heavy
brass railing gleamed but a fingertip away. He lunged for it, grabbing the slippery railing with both hands. His grip tightened as he
slid the lower part of his body between the railing and the deck and
into the cold, dark waters of the Sabine River. For a moment he
panicked. He would freeze to death! But his instinct for survival
calmed him. He was almost twelve years old, and he had swum in
colder waters. He would swim in this.

Releasing his grip on the railing, he pushed off with both feet
from the sloping side of the ship. The incoming tide swept his unre-
sisting body into its path and toward the stern of the vessel. Terrified
at the strength of the racing current, he stretched his arms in strong
arcs, surfacing. He paddled furiously, kicking with his feet to escape
the undertow created by the large paddlewheel at the stern. Noises

from the wheel muffled his own splashing. He had to stay on the surface. He could not fight the pull of the deeper water in the channel.

For the first time in his life he was grateful for his black skin, now a perfect camouflage in the murky waters. One more surge and he had cleared the wake of the fast-moving steamer. He paused and began to tread water as he looked about to get his bearings. His chest ached. His breath came in sobbing gasps. His nose and throat burned from the salty water hitting his face. The tide was his enemy as it forced his bruised body through the strait.

Boy knew he must move fast or be tossed onto the oyster reef that separated the Texas channel from the Louisiana channel. On the trip before, when first he planned his escape, he had decided he must not be trapped in either one. He had to get ashore in the unsettled area south of the channels. He had guessed he would have to swim about a quarter of a mile to reach shore.

He dared not use his feet on the surface. Using a scissors kick, he swam with the tide toward the Texas coast. He was a good swimmer. Massa Richard had taught him so that he might watch over his son, Young Massa Richard. The thin streak of light on the horizon heralded the approach of day. Twice he looked back over his shoulder at the blockade runner steaming toward the Gulf of Mexico, trying under the cover of darkness to slip past the Union ship anchored off Sabine Pass.

Good, he thought. *The lookout is busy. He did not see me leave the ship.*

Except for the stinging pain in the calf of his leg, Boy was almost enjoying the swim. His exertions had sent the warming blood through his body, and the cold water no longer bothered him. Yet the nagging fear of what lay ahead kept him from fully savoring these first moments of freedom.

The knowledge of the mudflat he would have to cross before reaching the safety of dry land now worried him. He shuddered at the thought of being caught in its stinking grip like a cow in a bog. He turned over on his back and floated, resting his tired limbs.

When his teeth began to chatter, he once more struck out vigorously toward the shoreline. Soon he was able to dog-paddle as he searched for a break in the tall grasses guarding the beach.

A small bay, sheltered from the tide, appeared. The water was now placid, with only slow-moving, shallow swells to indicate the incoming tide. Dawn brightened the sky, and he could clearly see the gray marsh grasses through the saw weeds. Where was the mud-stained, sandy beach he had seen before? He knew there was a white shell road about thirty feet inland from the beach, too. He had seen it from the upper deck of the ship. Cautiously, he thrust his foot down, testing for bottom. Ugh! He jerked it back from the gooey silt, and gave a swift thrust forward. Both feet slapped at the surface of the water.

I'm almost there, he thought. *I'm going to make it. Yes, sir, I've done it.*

The excitement of running away from his new owner no longer buoyed him. His arms were aching, and his legs felt as though he had climbed mountains. Nauseated from the salt water he'd swallowed, his stomach rolled in rebellion. How different it was from the river he had usually swum in at Green Gates. And the difference reminded him he was now alone, hungry, and in strange waters off an unfamiliar shore.

The water became too shallow for swimming. Gingerly he let his feet drop into the mud as he prepared to walk to dry land. Mud oozed between his toes as he began to sink into the softness. He was not tall, only a little over five feet. When his feet finally rested on firm bottom, the muddy silt was at his waist and the water at his armpits. He was grateful the mud didn't clutch like quicksand. It was just there. It had to be endured. Boy began to struggle forward. In his haste, he almost lost his balance. He had to watch it, take his time, or he would never see daylight again. He took comfort from hearing himself speak.

Slowly he moved forward, hampered by his constant fear of stepping on a crab, or encountering a snake, or stepping into a waterhole in the mud. His movements were dreamlike as he made his way on tiptoe, swinging from side-to-side, weaving through the mud.

Soon he was out of the water but still knee-deep in the wide mudflat. His mind, now numbed by fear and exhaustion, offered one thought—*keep on walking*. He could see tufts of salt grass now protruding through the mud. From the roughness of the bottom, he knew he was nearing firmer land. A movement in the rushes near him caught his eye. He scrambled forward, his knees now clear of the mud. In his haste to escape the varmint or snake near him, he tripped over his feet and fell. This section of the mudflat was shallower. He was able to push himself up from the mud that momentarily covered his face. He spit and sputtered and attempted to wipe the rank-smelling stuff from his lips and nose. Forgetting his hands, too, were mud-covered, he made matters worse. He began sobbing aloud in his disgust.

When at last he reached the firm sand, he fell to his knees and began to retch. In a frenzy of despair, he tore his wet shirt from his back and tried to clean his face. Stagnant pools left by a higher tide were the only water at hand. He had no choice. He could not stand the stench of his sickness. Wringing the brackish water from his shirt, he used it to wipe his face. The water smelled of dead fish, and it was all he could do to keep from throwing up again.

He stood up, finally, and looked about him. First, he spotted his owner's cotton-clad steamer about to clear Sabine Pass. From the corner of his eye, he noted the approach of the gray-painted Union blockader as it steamed toward the smaller Confederate ship. By its size, he knew it to be the Yankee warship, *Owasco*. The men on the docks at Beaumont complained of its harassment. He watched long enough to see the cotton-clad swing about in a sharp turn and head back up the channel. Smoke belched from its smoke stack. Boy realized it was now light enough for the sailors to see him. He would have to hide. He turned inland and raced toward a clump of tall grass. This would shelter him until the ship passed on its way back to Beaumont.

Boy fell to the ground behind a knoll of grass and fainted from pain and exhaustion. As he drifted into unconsciousness, he was vaguely aware that his hand had brushed against a large cotton-mouth water moccasin as it slithered off into the mudflat. The snake didn't bite him, but the young boy did not know that either. He lay unconscious for a few moments. Finally he stirred, raised himself to a sitting position, and looked about, completely disoriented. The piercing blast from the ship's horn, taunting the blockader, shocked him to his senses. He hurtled backwards, remembering the clump of grass that had harbored the snake. The mixture of arms and legs rolling on the beach took form, and Boy stood up.

Every inch of his mud-covered body ached. Examining his hand, he found no snakebite. Flexing his fingers, he felt no pain. No swelling, either, only the same tiredness that permeated his entire body registered. Yet he knew he must go on. He must find a hiding place. The senna bush offered little protection from the north side. It had shielded him from the ship's view as it passed on into the Texas channel and into the Sabine Lake, but soon there would be other boats in the channel. Fishermen, trappers, patrol boats, and even another blockade runner would try to make the Pass. He looked longingly at the deserted lighthouse across the channel on the Louisiana side. Sabine Pass was not lighted now. The United States would have to depend on renegade Texas bar pilots to guide their vessels safely through the shallow strait guarding the approaches to the deeper harbors of Orange and Beaumont, Texas. He turned to study the coastline. To the south, a sea of grass separated him from the small town of Sabine City and the new Fort Griffin to the north.

He dropped to a crouch, wanting to think. Had he wasted his time? Was this all he had to show for his break to freedom? From others he had heard of the "underground railroad" set up to help negro slaves escape to the north. But he had no one to trust or direct him in escaping. He had not dared question the slaves on the docks. Since the War began, everyone was suspicious or afraid to talk. Boy had witnessed the beating of two freedom-seeking blacks following their capture in East Texas. The men were marked for life by the beatings they received. Boy hunched lower, trying vainly to blend into the drab March landscape.

A brisk wind was now ruffling the grasses. Was it the beginning of a dreaded Texas norther? Boy wondered if northers blew in in the spring. Since coming to Beaumont from Georgia, he had heard of the sudden drop in temperature and the harsh, cold winds out of the Panhandle. He had not been in Texas long enough to experience one.

Oh, Lordy, he moaned, *send me some shelter. Hide me, Lord, please.* He opened his eyes. The light was better now.

What he had mistaken for tall grass to the north and a little west of him now appeared to be a low, man-made levee. The white oyster shell road to the town lay between him and the wall of dirt. He hurried toward it, bent over double, still wary of being discovered. He came to the road and looked up and down for a crossing place. Since the road was built on a slight rise, he knew he would be visible to any of the townspeople who might be looking in his direction. He decided to follow its curving length from the shallow drainage ditch on the water's side. He could hear faint sounds of the town stirring by the time he was opposite the wall he had spotted.

Still bent as low as possible, he dashed across the road, like a large mud-caked bug in awkward flight. In a moment, he was behind the embankment of the old, ruined Fort Griffin. He had found his hiding place. Boy straightened to his full height and moved about, checking his position. There was little left of the old battery, for that was all it appeared to have been. It was not like the fancy ramparts he had seen in New Orleans on the trip to deliver Massa Richard's cotton. And in Atlanta . . . But he shook his head in an effort to dislodge those memories. Boss Jordan, his new owner, had not permitted such favors. That was only one more reason why Boy knew he would never go back.

Boy found one cavelike structure in the side of the bastion. A few wooden boxes used for storing ammunition lay nearby, their broken lids exposing their emptiness. He sighed. Had he expected to find food and water to drink?

"Ah needs a fire." Even as he spoke aloud to the unhearing walls, he realized he might freeze to death that night if he did not find a better shelter or a fire. He had survived his fear of drowning, sticking in the mud, and even being bitten by a snake. Now he could picture himself dying for lack of water and food or freezing to death. "Yeah, Boy, you did just fine. You done freed yourself into a pickle. Now, whatcha gonna do?"

Tears stung his eyes, a sob rose in his throat, and his wound continued throbbing as his words echoed in the partially destroyed bombshelter. At last, overcome by the events of his escape and demoralized at the thought of his unplanned future, he dropped to the ground and began beating it with his dirty fists.

If I could only catch me a nap, he thought, as he tired of attacking the packed dirt. *Maybe then, I could think what to do.* He searched for a moment, then found a spot in the sun. He curled up and quickly fell asleep.

Chapter 2

BETHEL BANKS finished sweeping the back steps of her home in Sabine City. She stood for a moment leaning on her broom, staring out toward the Gulf of Mexico, and watched the Union blockader steam toward its watchpost in the Gulf. When the curling smoke of the escaping Confederate cotton-clad left the strait and entered the Texas channel, her gaze swept again toward the Gulf. Something was moving on the road. A dark mass crossed the white shell road below old Fort Griffin. She straightened, shielding her eyes against the early rising sun.

It looked like the Fontenots' old black cow had jumped the fence again. She knew Marie and Thibeau were still too weak from the fever to go chasing their old muley cow. She would have to saddle Nell and go fetch the dratted animal. Why they kept her was more than Bethel could fathom. Dry nigh unto two years, that cow was too ornery to have a calf.

Bethel hung her broom on the rack on her back porch. Sid had carved the rack the year before, shortly before his death. Her work-worn hands caressed the carved wood surface of the crude holder as though she were making physical contact with her dead husband. The crowing of Red, her big rooster, halted her reverie. Time to go to the section house and get the feed for the chickens and turkeys.

"Well, Sid, here's another day beginning and it ain't getting any better. First Jed leaves, and then—" but she could not finish her sentence. She took a man's large handkerchief from her apron pocket. One loud snort and she was done with sentiment for the day. She had to quit talking to herself, too. Folks thought she was daft enough, as it was. Glancing about her, as though expecting to see an eavesdropper, she stretched, breathed deeply for a moment, then moved toward the gate to the chicken yard. The tangy, salt breeze, blowing in from the Gulf, ruffled the short curls escaping her starched dustcap.

One old busybody hen spotted her mistress at the gate and clucked her discovery to the rest of the flock. Bethel made a dash for the protection of the section house adjacent to the chicken yard and banged the door shut between her and the advancing flock of chickens and turkeys. Several enterprising pullets tried to follow her by way of the too-small glassless windows. They fell back, with feathers flying, among the noisy flock. Bethel reached her hand through one of the windows and threw a handful of corn as far out as she could. Then, grabbing a filled bucket with each hand, she set off, ahead of the birds, toward the feed troughs.

Sagging, paint-chipped pickets surrounded the two-acre tract that made up the chicken yard. Here and there she had improvised to strengthen the fence, but her improvements did nothing to enhance the overall appearance. Worn railroad ties leaned in different directions for bracing. Pieces of sheet metal, salvaged from the buildings damaged by the Union barrage the year before, replaced missing pickets. But the fence served its purpose. And well it did, for raising chickens and turkeys was the widow's only source of income, other than her baking.

Yellow fever had swept through Texas the year before, taking her husband, Sid, in its terrible wake. He had died the month before the Union ships had fired on Sabine City. That had been October of 1862. The Union victory had been short-lived. Galveston Island and Sabine City were recaptured by the Confederacy the following January.

She had little time for grieving. Her business was brisk with the coming of the Davis Guards to the new Fort Griffin being constructed at the Point. Lieutenant Dick Dowling and the hotel now contracted for all her eggs and most of her poultry. After Dowling's arrival, and upon discovering the appetites of the men under his command, she had sent to Beaumont for turkeys to supplement her flock of chickens.

As she dumped the last bit of grain from her buckets, she decided she would fill the water troughs the next day. Yesterday's shower had freshened them enough for another day.

"All right, Sister Sue, let's have none of that!" She tossed an over-nosey Rhode Island hen from under her ruffled petticoat. Miz Banks loved her chickens. She tolerated the awkward, gawky turkeys.

She remembered how Sid had laughed at her plans to become a chicken farmer, but he had used the section crew to build the fence. As she put setting after setting under her obliging hens, he had teased her about "planning on feeding an army." That had been only three years ago, during the fall of '60. Bethel could not explain her feelings of foreboding, akin to the dreams of Pharoah in old Egypt. She had sensed an urgency in the air—a need to make ready for changes. She felt she must increase her stock and fill her larder. This she had done, even though her family's numbers had dwindled since she and Sid had come with the railroad to Texas. Both daughters had married sweethearts in Buffalo, their former home.

Her older son had gone out west with the railroad and Jed, her baby, had come to Texas with them when Sid had the offer from the Eastern Texas Railroad. Now Sid was dead. Jed had escaped the Confederate draft of April of 1862 by following his brother out west. So she was alone, a transplanted Yankee, trying to make Texas her home. Her neighbors were not unfriendly but reserved, knowing her outspoken sentiments for the preservation of the Union.

Bethel closed the door to the old railroad section house she had converted into a storeroom. Next to it stood the water tank. A shell from one of the Yankee ships had knocked down part of its underpinning. With the help of the Fontenots, she had been able to saw through the damaged timbers. Its top gone, the tank now rested on the ground like a tipsy tub. She could easily dip water out of it for her stock. The pipe from the well was mounted over it so that she had no problem keeping the tank full with the help of the windmill.

Like the cypress tank, the barn tilted crazily to one side. It, too, had caught a cannonball in its roof. But her home was undamaged.

She had much to be thankful for, she thought, as she surveyed her small domain that morning.

Her inspection completed, she walked toward the house scattering chickens in front of her. Like all the other wooden buildings along the Gulf Coast in that area, her house needed painting. Functional in design, as plain and unpretentious as its owner, it was two stories high, sported two dormers, and had a chimney at each end of the house. The front porch and the back porch ran the width of the house. On top of the hipped roof was a small widow's walk. She had insisted on the widow's walk. Sid had huffed and puffed at the additional expense, saying they had no use for it. Bethel, remembering her childhood in Maine, wanted this reminder of her roots.

She loved to watch the approaching storms from her widow's walk. She missed the crash of the big breakers along the stony New England coast. How she had hated it when her father had moved them to Buffalo! After an accident at sea, he was no longer fit to sail the whaling ships. He had piloted one of the flat-bottomed boats on Lake Erie until his death.

Now Bethel's love of the sea had tied her to Sabine City, even after her husband's death. She found she could make a living by providing poultry and eggs and daily orders of freshly baked bread, breakfast and dinner rolls, and pastries for Mrs. Dorman's hotel. *Rolls!* She ran toward the house. Her angular figure resembled a modishly dressed scarecrow flapping in the breeze. It must be eight o'clock, and she hadn't set the dinner rolls to rising!

The large kitchen was tidy and warm. Her breakfast dishes were drying on the drainboard of the wooden sink. She washed and dried her hands, using the homespun towel hanging on the rack. Pushing back her long sleeves, she carried the huge wooden flour bowl over to the well-scrubbed table that once was the map table in the section house. From a cabinet drawer, she lifted an oversized rolling pin. She unfolded the heavy piece of ship's canvas and secured it to the table with four quilting frame clamps. Now she was ready.

She could hardly lift the crockery bowls holding the masses of puffy dough. There were three of them at the end of the table. Large pans were greased and stacked by the iron bakery stove. The stove was paid for with her first poultry profits. She had sent all the way to St. Louis for it. Sid had had a fit when he saw the bill of lading. But the first fruitcakes she baked in it had changed his mind. Checking the fire, she grinned at the memory of his reaction to her first order of cordwood for the stove. How he had ranted!

"I'm running a railroad down here and my wife has her supplies shipped in by water!" The section hands had doubled over with laughter knowing, as he did, the ribbing he would take in the saloon when word got around. She had been apologetic and certainly had not meant any harm when she had ordered the wood. It had seemed such a bargain at the time. Now, since the railroad was no longer in operation, all her supplies came by steamer.

By nine o'clock she had covered the pans of rolls with clean towels and cleared the wide worktable. She refolded the canvas and placed it in the long drawer under the table. The drawer once held grade and bridge drawings for the now defunct Eastern Texas Railway. She checked the oven once more. The fires were glowing and expertly banked from the four o'clock breakfast baking. She had more than an hour to busy herself before it was time to bake the dinner rolls. As she dried her hands, she stared out the kitchen window, her eyes gazing toward the Gulf. And it was then she remembered that dratted cow!

She could not see Black Magic—what a name for an old barren cow, and what a waste of time. But the Fontenots would fret if they didn't hear her bellowing soon. Two shrill whistles from Bethel brought Nell, the black mare, up from the back fence, scattering chickens and turkeys from her path. Bethel removed the tarp covering the saddle on the sawhorse on the back porch. The saddle belonged in the barn or the section house, but she got tired of having to traipse out there to saddle the mare when she needed her.

Nell stood easy as Bethel swung the saddle into position over the blanket. A few seconds passed before she was satisfied with the rigging. She took her worn cape from the peg in the kitchen and draped it around her shoulders. *Wouldn't do to take pleurisy.* Then with a grunt, she swung into the saddle. She sat astride, like a man, her skirts voluminous enough to hide her long, bony legs. Her black cape lay about her. She secured her dustcap to her heavy thatch of gray hair before reaching for the reins tied around the post of the porch. Then she was off.

She loved to ride. She did not care how ungainly she appeared on the short-legged Morgan horse. As long as she was not improper, she did not care what the townspeople thought. She rode through the town, nodding and waving as circumstances indicated. She slowed the horse as she passed the town's business area and came in sight of the Irish soldiers working on the little earthenworks being built on the land jutting out into the channel. She could hear them grumbling among themselves as they lifted the heavy pieces of iron rails to form the center of the U-shaped fort. Above the quaint and earthy calls of the men could be heard the clipped, Austrian-accented commands of Colonel Sulakowski, the engineer-in-charge.

They are the moaningest bunch of men I have ever known—and the

workingest, she thought to herself. She believed in giving the devil his due. Not that these men of the Jeff Davis Guards were devils, although they might sound like devils on payday—she knew them to be good-hearted men. Most of the town had expected the Stewart house, where they were billeted, to be in shambles by now. But no damage to matter had occurred. Captain Odlum and young Dowling held a tight rein on the former dockworkers from Galveston.

Nell began to trot after passing Fort Griffin. The crisp breeze heightened the widow's color in the short time it took to reach the site of old Fort Sabine. Abandoned after the October '62 shelling, it was now a fraction of its former size. Colonel Griffing had been wise in moving to another, more strategic location, she thought.

Now where is that old muley cow? If she's stuck in the mud behind a clump of grass—then good riddance. She dismounted, not caring if her long, stockinged legs showed. She called, "Blackie, come here." She whistled through her teeth in an effort to mimic Fontenot's way of calling the pet cow in from the pasture. But no answering "Moo" could be heard.

Just as she figured. Blackie was hiding down behind that mound of dirt. Bethel struggled back into the saddle and arranged her clothes before urging Nell through the reeds in the drainage ditch and up the grassy bastion. The horse reached the top without too much effort. Scanning the waving tall grasses around the perimeter of the fort, Bethel saw no black cow. She was turning the horse to leave when she spotted the mud-covered mass that was Boy curled up at the entrance to the ammunition cellar. At first she thought it was a dead animal. But something about its position made her move her horse to a better vantage point. A pesky mosquito or perhaps the angry wound on Boy's leg began to trouble him. He stirred in his sleep.

"It's a human being, and it's alive!"

Chapter 3

A WOMAN'S VOICE! Boy tried to open his mud-caked eyes, but the effort was almost too much for him. The mud had dried and almost sealed them shut. He sat up and began rubbing his eyes. The woman gasped and the horse nickered as though it, too, had been frightened by the mud-covered boy at the bottom of the slope.

"You! You down there. Speak up. Who are you? Where do you stay?" At the sound of those nasal commands from what looked like one of the creatures described in stories around the campfire in the compound of Green Gates, Boy obeyed. He stood up, shivering from the encounter more than from the chilly, morning shadows now engulfing him.

"I'm Boy," he muttered truculently, his eyes searching for a way to escape.

It was useless, he thought. *That old grass is full of snakes and there sits an old witch on a horse. I'm done for.* His kinky head hung down, his body and spirit awaiting the blows he felt sure would begin to fall on his naked back. Why had he promised his mother he'd try to get free?

Mother's wish

She had been a frail woman, too weak to do heavy field work. When they sold his father, she seemed to make no effort to get over the flu. "You've got to be free," she had urged him over and over in her feverish state. He would never forget that night or what she had said. He had decided right then that when he was sixteen he would try to run away. Now he was almost sorry. What would happen to him?

"Don't just stand there. You! I'm talking to you. Didn't your mammy teach you any respect for your elders?"

At the word *mammy*, he felt the tears begin to well up under his eyelids.

"You look at me when I speak to you." She urged the horse down the slope to where he stood.

She had his attention now. He had never heard a woman speak in such sharp, cut-off words before. The white ladies he had known had soft, quiet voices that sort of sang out the words. Not this one. *Maybe—well, I ain't no coward. I might as well ask and be done for.* "Is you a witch, Ma'am?"

"A witch? Me? Is that what I look like to you?"

He stepped back, dumbfounded, for the "witch" began to chuckle. It was a happy sound that seemed to surround him with its cheeriness.

She paused, evidently aware of his fright for the first time. "Son, don't be afraid. I'm just an old white widow woman looking for a black muley cow. Come up here, closer. I want to talk to you. I won't hurt you."

He moved toward her, noticing for the first time the sharp, shooting pains in the calf of his leg where the anchor point had cut. He took a few more steps and paused a minute, waiting for the wave of pain to subside.

"What's wrong, son? Why are you dragging your leg? Are you a cripple?" There was concern for him in her voice, and he was no longer afraid.

"No'm. Cut myself." He reached the horse's side and looked up at his interrogator. He did not know what a ludicrous sight he made, covered from head to toe in dried mud a shade lighter than his skin.

"How'd you cut yourself? Where is it? And how did you get so muddy?" He watched without answering as the tall woman with the billowing clothes dismounted the small horse. The wind was blowing strong from the Gulf, whipping her clothes about the two of them. He looked up at her and began to sniffle.

"Can't say, Ma'am. I'se running away." Would she take him to the men with the fierce dogs? Nothing ever went right for him. First they had sold his pappy to the sugarcane man. Then his mammy had died. When Young Massa Richard had told the lie about him, they had sold him to the boatman, Boss Jordan. At least no one had beat him yet. If only, he wished forlornly, Massa Richard had believed him and punished the true culprit, Young Massa Richard. The white boy had ridden his pet pony to death and then told his father Boy did it. Massa had believed his son, and Boy left Green Gates, the only home he had known.

"Well, I don't see anything but mud. Where is it?" The woman was bending down, looking for his wound. He pushed his injured leg in her direction. "Yes. It's bad. I can tell by the swelling—but that's all. We've got to get that mud off before we do anything else." She straightened and placed her warm hand on his shoulder. "You're cold, too, aren't you? Where's your shirt?"

She was scolding him, but she did not sound mean. Maybe she wouldn't turn him in. He looked up, not speaking but fighting hard to keep from crying. His thin chest rose up and down and its movement caught her eye. "You'll have to come home with me and get cleaned up and doctored. Bet you haven't eaten lately, either."

That did it. The mention of food chased all thoughts of escape from his mind. He would go with her and accept his punishment. Once more his shoulders slumped as though the blows from an overseer's bullwhip were beating down on him, even now.

"Don't you faint on me. Here, I'll put my hands around your waist while you push off with your good foot and we'll have you behind the saddle in no time." Her words were hearty and cheerful.

Meekly he followed her instructions and was soon perched behind the saddle.

She gave a sigh, then stood back from the horse. "Son, we've got a problem."

He turned his big, questioning eyes toward her.

"I forgot I've got to get on the horse, too. And with all these clothes. Wonder when they will make decent clothes for womenfolk to wear on horseback?" She paused as if studying the situation. "All right, young fellow. This is the way it'll have to be. You lie back over Nell's rump and put your hands over your eyes and don't peek. You stay that way until I tell you to sit up. Understand?"

He shrugged his shoulders and obeyed, lying back and placing his dirty hands tightly over his eyes. Maybe she was a witch. Maybe she was going to make him disappear. He no longer cared, not knowing what would happen to him once they got into town. He could not see her as she placed one shoe in the stirrup, and with a mighty swing, threw her leg and all its coverings of petticoats, dress, and cape over his reclining figure and to the other side of the horse. She wiggled a bit until she was satisfactorily settled in the saddle. Then she reached back and pulled her skirts from on top of the boy and into position, down her side, covering both her legs and his.

"Sit up, now. Hug the saddle as close as you can. I'm going to spread my cape out over you and tuck you in so folks won't be asking foolish questions. We'll decide what needs to be done when you and I get to the house."

"Yes'm. Yes, Ma'am!" There was surprise and joy in his voice. *She's going to help me.* Hope surged through his battered body once more.

"Humpf! Don't get all excited. You're a long way from being out of this mess. We're going back through town, and I hope no one has seen us. Will you be all right?" She half turned in the saddle.

"Yes'm," came his muffled answer.

"Tuck that cape under your backside so it doesn't blow free." He complied, and then they were off at a smooth trot as he clung to the back of the saddle with all his might.

Once she stopped and passed the time of day with a man who asked her about her chickens. Boy was relieved when she told the man goodby. "Sorry to have to rush, Simonet. I've got to get my rolls into the oven." He heard a shout of greetings and felt she must have waved, for she hit him in the head as she grabbed for the elusive edge of the cape that had fluttered when she moved her hand. "Oh dear," she sighed deeply, as she whispered to him. "My cape almost got away. I'll have to seem unfriendly until we reach the house. It's too risky, stopping or waving." In his heart, he thanked her. He was still puzzled that a white woman would go to this much trouble for him.

He could tell by the sound of the horse's hooves they had left the shell road and were on grass. Wonder where she was taking him? It was not long before he knew. He was in a barn. He could smell the hay and feed. She pulled the cape off of him, and his eyes began to adjust to the bright sunlight coming in over him. *In a barn? Sunlight from the sky?* He hastily raised his eyes and saw half the roof of the barn was missing. He looked about but had no time to ask questions.

She was staring at him as she twisted in the saddle for a better view. "We've got to get that mud off you so I can tell if you're smart or stupid. Can't help you if you're a know-it-all or a smart aleck."

His eyes fell before her fierce glare. He bit his lip and got dirt in his teeth. He wanted to spit but did not dare. What was she going to do with him?

In answer to his unspoken question, she said, "Can you climb down from here without hurting your leg?" She watched as he held onto the back of the high saddle and slid to the ground. He spotted a bale of hay, hopped over to it and sat down. She nodded her approval.

"You stay here and I'll be back in a minute with food and water."

Food! He would not budge an inch. He would take root to the spot if it meant getting a cold biscuit. He watched her ride out of the barn, wondering if and when she would be back. While he waited, he rubbed his aching leg and looked at the inside of the barn. There was not much left of it. A remnant of the roof provided enough cover for a stall and a rack of shelves. Bales of hay were stacked under the damaged portion. There was enough of the barn to shelter a horse and a cow or two. He wondered what had happened to the roof. Most likely a hurricane, he reasoned. Then he noticed the fowl in the yard. Never before had he seen so many chickens and turkeys. Green Gates had a lot of chickens, what with all the mouths to feed. Besides the white folks, there were grown slaves and all their children. This old lady must have a powerful lot of slaves, he thought. But where were the quarters? Why hadn't she

turned him over to his own kind for safekeeping? She's different, he
thought. What had he let himself in for, leaving Boss Jordan and
his crew?

His pulse quickened at the sound of footsteps coming his way.
He crouched behind the bale and held his breath. But it was only
the old woman. In one hand she carried a black kettle, and in the
other, a napkin-covered plate. Fried meat! He could smell the meat
from where she stood in the doorway. She was looking about her as
if for something she had misplaced.

"Now, drat it, where's that old milk bucket?" He looked and
spotted it behind one of the bales of hay.

"There, Ma'am," he pointed. He climbed back to his seat on
the hay.

"Good." She walked over to him and set the plate by his side.
"No, no," she cautioned. "Don't you touch that until you've washed

your face and hands. You've got enough trouble with an infected leg." His stomach groaned, but he did not protest. He hobbled over where she was pouring water into a bucket. She handed him a rag she had thrown over her arm.

"Now, Son, wash your hands good, and clean your face. I know you're hungry—but you have to eat clean. I ought to make you bathe, first—" She began to chuckle when she saw the look on his face. "No, I'm not that mean."

"Now, let me put some fresh water in that bucket," she said as she threw the dirty water out toward the chicken yard. He obediently rinsed his hands and face. Would he starve before his appearance suited the old witch? She seemed to be able to read his thoughts, for she grinned and handed him the towel. As soon as he dried his face and hands, she motioned him over toward the plate of food. He wolfed down a biscuit and reached for the piece of fried pork. He began to tear at it with his teeth before he noticed the knife and fork beside the plate on the hay. He waited for her disapproval, but from the corner of his eye, he saw she was gazing at the chickens and not watching him at all.

"Cup your hands," she ordered. He did, in time to receive the last of the cool water from the kettle. He got most of it to his mouth, and promptly finished the meat and the remaining biscuit. His face radiated gratitude as he sat back on the bale of hay and looked up at her, waiting for her next move.

"Thank you, Ma'am," he mumbled. Her sharp eyes noted his empty plate, and the quietness now registered on his face.

"We've got to figure out a way to get that leg and the rest of you clean. And I've got to see to my baking." Her brows puckered in thought. "I want you to go out to the water tank and scrub as much of that mud off as possible before I take you into the house. But I don't want any of the neighbors seeing you and asking questions. Let me see," she said, pushing back the dustcap she was wearing and scratching her head.

"I know. I'll lead Nell over to the tank, and you can walk on the other side of her, and they won't see you. I want you stripped down and bathed clean as a whistle when I get back with some of my boy Jed's clothes. Good thing I kept them. I knew they would come in handy one day. Now, do you understand?" Even as she asked, she walked over to one of the shelves and took down a large bar of lye soap.

"Yes'm." He got up and stood at the entrance to the barn as she whistled Nell up from the yard.

"Keep your head down," she cautioned. She lived at the end of the road and had no neighbors on the railroad side. She tied the bridle to the post by the tank before standing by the horse, her back turned to him. "Now remember. Keep your head down. I'll be back as soon as I put my rolls to bake and locate the clothes."

Boy, hidden from any outsider's view by the horse and the woman's skirts, pulled his ragged trousers off and crawled over the side of the tank. Bethel turned and walked rapidly toward her kitchen.

Using the rag she had given him and the strong-smelling lye soap, he began to scrub his muddy body. The soap stung the cut, and he wanted to yell. But he did not. He was grateful the sun had had time to take the chill off the water in the tank. He even washed his hair, moving about in the tank to keep the suds from getting into his eyes. Finally he was cleaner than he had ever been in his life. The water felt good to his sore leg, and he splashed about, enjoying it. He remembered to keep his head below the top of the tank.

But he soon tired, and goose pimples covered his body. Then he heard her footsteps. He got as close to the side of the tank as he could to hide his nakedness. *She's a crazy old woman, and I don't want her looking at me,* he thought. But she stopped on the far side of the horse and stood with her back to the tank.

"Quick, now. Get out and dry off. I'll stay here on this side and folks, if they're watching, won't see you for my skirts." He crawled over the side and grabbed for the pants, pulling them on so quickly he hurt his leg. He stifled the moan as best he could. He did not want her to turn and ask what was the matter. Then he took the coarse towel and dried the rest of himself.

"Aren't you ready, yet?"

"Yes'm."

"Good. Now, we'll walk back to the far side of the house. I left the window open and you can squeeze through it into the bedroom. I'm afraid the Fontenots will see you if I take you through the back door."

"Yes'm."

"Is that all you can say, 'yes'm'?" Her tone was sharp for the first time.

He did not know what she wanted him to say, so he tried once more. "Yes, Ma'am."

"Oh, you're polite enough. I meant, say anything to make conversation."

"I ain't never talked to no white lady before, Ma'am," he tried not to show his anxiety.

"We'll fix that, then."

"How, Ma'am?"

"Oh, never mind. Get that worried look off your face. Here we are. Come around on this side of the horse and I'll give you a boost." He did. She boosted him up so he could crawl through the window. His leg was aching and he sat down on the floor, just inside the white curtained window.

Never before had he been inside a white folks bedroom. Everything's all white, he noticed. White curtains, white bedcovers, white rock tabletop. Even the walls were white. He stared at the pictures of the white men and the two white boys hanging on the wall. Black folks did not have pictures of their kin to hang on the walls of their cabins. A longing for his mammy rose in his throat and threatened to choke him. Tears welled in his eyes. It wasn't fair, being a black boy and a slave and being so alone. But the strident voice of the widow woman calling to him from the kitchen reminded him he certainly was not alone anymore. *And that may be worse than ever,* he thought. *But if I don't get killed for running away this time, I'm going to do it again. I got to be free, but this time, if I can, I'm going to make me a plan.*

Chapter 4

"COME IN the kitchen and talk to me while I take my rolls from the oven," the widow woman called through the doorway. He stood up and limped painfully into the kitchen. And what a kitchen! Besides the cook stove, it had an iron oven built into the brick wall that was once the fireplace. There was a large table in the middle of the room. China cabinets lined one wall. On the wall next to the porch was a long wooden sink with a hand pump. White muslin curtains trimmed in a colorful fringe covered the short windows over the sink. A rocking chair was in the far corner, flanked by three comfortable chairs. On a small round table near the rocker were a big lamp, a sewing basket, and a black-bound book.

Boy watched the woman take big pans of something from the oven. He knew the oven was hot because she used huge, padded holders to remove the pans. The kitchen was warm and had a delicious aroma. The objects in the pans looked like biscuits, but Boy could tell they were not. And they didn't smell like biscuits. They smelled like the white bread the white folks at Green Gates ate. She turned in time to see him sniffing the air.

"Like it?" she asked.

"Like what, Ma'am?"

"The smell of my rolls."

"Rolls?"

She leaned against the sink and surveyed him. "Come here," she ordered. He moved to where she stood, wondering what she wanted. She looked at him a moment and pulled out a chair, motioning for him to sit down. She walked out on the back porch and brought a bowl of butter back with her. Picking up two of the hot rolls, she quickly buttered them and placed them on a plate in front of the boy. "Try those." When she saw he did not understand her command, she said, "Eat them."

He relished the pure joy of tasting white yeast bread and butter, oblivious of the butter running down the corners of his mouth. His mammy had slipped him some stale cake several times, but those fading memories did not compare with the flavor of the rolls. She smiled as she handed him a cup of milk and another buttered roll.

"Those are rolls, just small, individual loaves of white bread."

"They're good, white lady. Real good."

"My name, young man, is Bethel Banks. You may call me 'Miz Banks' like everyone else in town does."

"Yes'm." And suddenly there was a rumble of wheels leaving the road and rolling on grass.

"Quick, get into the bedroom." Miz Banks grabbed him by the arm and almost pushed him into the room. "Be real quiet and don't open this door."

Boy's eyes were wide with fright. Who was coming?

"Come in, Moses." Her voice sounded shaky but cheerful as she greeted the elderly black man who belonged to Mrs. Dorman and worked at the hotel. "The rolls are ready. Have you all been busy today?"

"Yes'm. The crew from the *Hamilton* was in and out all morning drinking coffee. They lost themselves a black boy. He done jumped ship. They missed him when they got back to the docks. Now, they done be looking for him around the docks and the hotel."

"Whose boy is he? Did he fall off the steamer?" They were talking about him. Would she tell? He cowered in the chair, straining to hear each word even though he knew flight was impossible.

"No'm, he didn't fall. Like I said, he done jumped. He belonged to Boss Jordan. Only had him a month. Got him from a planter up Georgia way."

"Did he jump into the water or run away while the boat was being loaded?"

"They don't rightly know, Miz Banks. He hadn't given them no trouble. Ain't whupped him none, they claim." Boy could hear the widow and the man loading the pans of rolls into the handcart.

When the handcart began to rumble over the rough yard beside the house, and then out into the street, he sighed, wondering if she would hide him forever, or if she would grow tired of being kind and call the sheriff.

The door opened to the bedroom, and he faced the fierce eyes of the woman he knew to be Miz Banks. Her long, bony face had a sadness about it. "Well," she said, "at least you didn't lie to me about running away." He straightened at the word *lie*.

"I don't lie, Ma'am, never!" He spoke with a force that seemed to surprise her.

"Well, now. That's better. I see you do have some spirit. Guess all that mud covered it up. What's your name?"

"They calls me 'Boy.'"

"That can't be your name. What'd your mammy call you?"

"She called me Boy, too. Young Massa Richard said to. So they did." He tried not to let her see his embarrassment at being name-less. It had not bothered him before.

"What do you want to be called? Every human being is entitled to a name."

"Even a slave boy like me?"

"Especially a slave boy like you. What else can you own but your good name?"

"Yes'm."

"Well?"

"Well, what, Ma'am?" He stood up, distressed at the change in her voice.

She pushed him back into the chair. "Do sit down. I want to know what to call you. Surely you know what you would like to be called?"

"No'm." Now that danger of discovery was past, his brain re-fused to function. His head felt hot, and he was cold and ached all over. She did not seem to notice.

"So, you never had enough gumption to name yourself, even in secret?" Her voice turned scornful. "Well, you were muddy when I found you, and now you're clean, but your mind's still muddy. When you start using that God-given intelligence you seem to possess and come up with a worthy name, I'll accept it. But until you do, you'll be known as Muddy Boy Banks around here." She whirled on her heel and flounced through the bedroom door.

She's mad at me 'cause I didn't name myself, mourned Boy. He had never thought it important, before. He knew it must be important to white folks, though. She said he'd be called Muddy Boy Banks until he could think of a better name. For a moment, he did try to think of a name. But she was right, his brain was filled with mud. He could not think. His leg was throbbing, and he felt miserable. He slid out of the chair and curled up in a ball on the worn braided rug. In a moment or two he was asleep. Only once was he conscious of any movement in the room. He felt the touch of a soft hand on his forehead and the warmth of a quilt being draped around him as he drifted into deeper sleep.

Chapter 5

DOCTOR MURRAY looked up from his cluttered desk when the Widow Banks walked into his office with a napkin-covered dish. He stood up, made an attempt to hide his welcoming grin with his hand, and cleared a chair for his visitor. *What could she be wanting this time of morning?* he wondered.

"Good morning, Doctor Murray." She set the dish on the desk and folded her hands primly in her lap as she sat in the chair.

"Is it? I hadn't noticed. I've been too busy."

"Don't you grumble and growl at me. I've forgiven you for your past behavior, and I've brought you some jellycake." She spoke matter-of-factly, as if their previous encounters had been mere disagreements, instead of loud and heated verbal battles.

"You forgive me? Why you are the one that called me—" He stopped fuming when she lifted the sweet-smelling cake and waved it under his nose.

"I know, I know. You can't help being the stubborn, prejudiced, old goat that you are. But you are a good doctor. And I need you." He grunted and pulled the plate of cake to him. "Now sit down and eat your jellycake before it gets cold. Where's your teapot?"

"Over there. You know good and well where it is. As many cups of tea as you have mooched—"

"Don't try my patience, Doctor. Sit down and hush. You're wasting my valuable time."

"Your time! What about my—?" But he hushed as she poured his tea. It was hard for him to sputter and eat the cake she had brought as an obvious bribe.

"Eat and hush your fretting. I know how overworked you are. But you have got to help me."

"You? You need my help? Why, you're as healthy as a horse. Don't come whining to me."

"It's not me, you old geezer. I've got an injured boy at my house. He's sick. He's got an infected leg. And," she leaned over the desk and whispered cautiously, "he's a black and a runaway."

"The boy off the *Hamilton*?"

"How'd you know?"

"I treated one of their men this morning for a broken finger he got in a fight with one of Dowling's Irishmen. He told me about the slave. Where'd you find him? How come you didn't turn him in?" Before she could answer, he hit the desk with his fist and shouted, "Now, that was a fool thing to ask, wasn't it? The whole town knows where your sympathies lie when it comes to slavery."

"I found him this morning behind the embankment of the old fort. I was out looking for the Fontenots' cow. And I don't intend turning him in. That was a fool question to ask." In spite of her tone of voice, her eyes spoke eloquently, begging the doctor for understanding and assistance.

"Now, Bethel, you know I can't conceal a runaway slave."

"I'm concealing him. I want you to treat him. Please," she added; her voice softened and she dropped her head. "He's so little and has no one. He'll die for sure if you turn him over to Boss Jordan."

"Jack Jordan's no villain. You know that."

"Yes, but we both know he can't give the boy proper care on that ship. We've got to protect him."

"What do you mean, *we*?"

"You're going to help me, aren't you? I know you don't like slavery any more than I do." She placed her hand on his sleeve, plainly begging.

The doctor finished his tea and cake. Then he got up and placed the empty dishes on a back table. He turned and towered over her. "We're at war, Madam. Slavery is only a small part of our disagreement with the Union. When the State of Texas seceded in '61, my sympathies went with the Confederacy."

"Don't preach to me." She stood up, almost as tall as he, and stared him in the face. "I know your sentiment. I have mine, too.

You know I consider this place my home. I intend to stay in Texas. I respect its rights, yet I hate slavery with all my being. And I didn't come down here for another battle with you." She calmed a bit as she saw him grin broadly. "Captain Odlum and his men are here to do what fighting has to be done. I came down here to get you to come treat a very sick boy. His color and ownership shouldn't even enter into it."

"I'm well aware of my duty as a doctor." But he smiled when he said it, and Bethel offered a smile of truce in return.

Did that mean he would help her? She watched as he leaned back in his swivel chair, apparently in deep thought. He looked at her, surprised to see tears running down her weathered face. "Now, now. None of that, Bethel. I never said I wouldn't come to see him. I merely said I wouldn't help you hide him from the authorities." He stood up and pulled on his coat. "Let's go see this miserable bit of flesh you've taken under your wing." He stopped, then grinned and patted her bony shoulder. "We'll think of something. I'd hate to have you in a good case of mullegrubs. Things would get boring around here if you lost your spark."

She climbed in the buggy beside him and settled herself and her skirts.

"Do you really—"

"Hush, I'm thinking. That's something you should have done before you took him in."

Urging the doctor to take the rig around to the far side of the house, she hoped the Fontenots would not notice. Perhaps they would think she was getting ready to go with the doctor to help him with a birthing, as she had done in the past. She knew nothing of midwifery, but he used her to bring order to the household while he delivered the baby. "The biggest difficulty in the average delivery is the inability of the doctor to cope with the family when he needs to devote all his time to the patient," the doctor had told her. He said it was her authoritative ways and Yankee efficiency that helped him.

Bethel showed Doctor Murray into the bedroom. Muddy still

lay curled up under the quilt on the braided rug. Doctor Murray dropped to his knees and began examining the young negro. Muddy stirred under the man's gentle probing and opened his eyes. He tried to twist away from the firm grip on his leg, but he had no strength.

"Whoa, there, boy," the kind voice said. "I'm not going to hurt you. I want to see what's wrong with you. Now lie still." Experienced hands moved over the boy's thin body. "Bethel, hand me that black ointment from my bag," the doctor instructed. "I'll need some wrappings for his leg, too. It looks clean enough, but we've got to get at that infection and make it start draining." She wasted no time in getting the supplies, then watched as he applied the ointment. "Don't worry, son; it won't stain," teased the doctor, in an effort to calm the frightened boy.

He finished wrapping the leg, using far more bandage than Bethel, who voiced her opinion, thought necessary. "Oh, hush. I know what I'm doing. Don't ask questions. Give me one more strip of cloth." She obediently tore another strip from the old sheet she was using to make the bandages. As he finished, Doctor Murray asked, "You going to keep him on the floor?"

For the first time, she thought about where she would keep Muddy. If he were well, she could keep him in the section house. But she did not want him out there alone until he was able to take care of himself. "I'll put him in Jed's bed upstairs." She reached down to pick up the slender figure, only to have the doctor stop her.

"Wait! I've got a notion. Leave him there for awhile. He'll be all right."

"But—"

"Come on now. This will take some doing. I need to wash up and be on my way as soon as possible." He gathered his belongings and repacked his bag. With a grunt, he stood up, then followed her out to the back porch. The washpan and lye soap were on a bench. She brought him hot water and a clean towel.

"When you finish, come on back into the kitchen. I know you'll not take time out for lunch, late as it is. And that jellycake was just a teaser. I'll have you some ham and eggs by the time the coffee is brewed." He didn't argue but sat at the table, resting his head on his arms. Bethel frowned, for she knew how overworked he was. Captain Bailey, the army doctor assigned to the post, was often out of town serving the other installations in the district. He dozed while she quietly prepared his food. What plan did he have, she wondered. She admired him and knew she could count on him to help her. The past January, when the newspaper printed what it termed "President Lincoln's notorious Emancipation Proclamation," she had been delighted. But Texas had not accepted it. She made the mistake of discussing her views with Doctor Murray. That was the last time she had seen him except to glimpse his buggy en route to business. At least he was still speaking to her. His temper matched hers, but she knew him to be a fair man.

She placed the plate of ham and eggs and hominy grits in front of him. A covered basket of warmed-over rolls was at his elbow. The coffee was steaming hot and fragrant in his cup when she touched his shoulder to awaken him.

"Oh, must have dozed off." His apology was unnecessary. Between mouthfuls, he outlined his plan for saving Muddy Banks.

Chapter 6

MUDDY BANKS slept on. He was unaware of being on the floor of the bedroom of Bethel Banks' house. After the doctor finished his meal, he prepared a laudanum potion. Then, he aroused the sick boy and made him drink the bitter brew. The doctor left after instructing Bethel in the part she would play upon his return.

Since Miz Banks' house stood near the docks, it was not long before the good doctor returned, accompanied by the burly captain of the *Hamilton*, Jack "Boss" Jordan. The two men stomped up on the back porch, pausing only long enough to scrape their boots. Bethel was reserved when she asked them to come into the house.

Doctor Murray began, "Miz Banks, this is Captain Jordan of the *Hamilton*." Both acknowledged the introduction. Doctor Murray strode toward the bedroom door and swung it open, revealing the curled-up and sleeping Muddy Banks.

"See for yourself, Jordan," the doctor waved his hand toward the recumbent figure. "I don't know if he will make it or not. He's unconscious." Bethel played her part well, too. Her face was drawn and sad. She reached down and removed the quilt, exposing the heavily-wrapped leg. The seaman walked over and prodded the drugged boy with one big, booted foot.

Doctor Murray shook his head. "Careful there."

Bethel's voice was sad and low, "He's so young."

Doctor Murray turned and eyed the captain. "I hope he didn't cost too much. You just might lose your investment."

"He cost me enough." Boss Jordan's booming voice filled the bedroom. Bethel silently prayed the potion had been strong enough to keep the boy asleep. They must have time to bargain for his

They trick Boss Jordan.

safety. "What's wrong with him? Looked and acted plenty healthy to me only yesterday."

"He's got malaria. He's running a high fever from that or that leg he cut in getting away from your ship. Don't know if we can save him or not. Needs to be taken to Beaumont to the hospital." The doctor's voice was serious. Bethel knew she must not laugh at his exaggerations. "Going to be expensive. But he's yours, isn't he?" Doctor Murray turned to Boss Jordan and stared intently at him.

"Got his bill of sale on board my ship. I ain't one to be using stolen merchandise. You know that."

"Sorry, Jordan. Didn't intend to offend. You do have a good reputation. I can tell you've not beaten him. Had him long?" *Good,* Bethel thought. *Let's find out all we can before Captain Jordan gets suspicious.*

"Got him after Christmas, when I was in Georgia. Some planter wanted to get rid of him, and rid of him fast. He seemed taken with the boy, however. But he offered me a bargain, and I took it. Cost me two hundred dollars."

"He's going to cost you a lot more before he's well. Or he may pull out of it with no trouble—unless it's a game leg." *Now, that's really skirting the truth,* thought Bethel. But she was grateful for the doctor's hedging, since the boy's welfare was at stake. Now it was her turn to speak.

"Captain, I would like to speak about the boy." He nodded for her to speak. "Let's leave him and go into the kitchen where we can talk." She turned toward the door. "Will you stay, Doctor Murray?"

"No, I've got to be on my way. But I'll look in on him tonight and find out what you plan to do with him. We can discuss my bill then, too, Captain Jordan." He hurried from the house.

She led the captain by the arm into the spicy-smelling kitchen. Pushing him in the direction of the chair at the table, she brought the coffeepot over from the cook stove. After pouring their coffee, she set a bowl of teacakes in front of the man. He nodded his appreciation as he began to eat one of the cookies. *Jordan,* she thought, *you're smart, but you're too trusting.* She knew better than to start sympathizing with him. She must think of what was best for Muddy.

"I was thinking, Captain Jordan—here, have another teacake— that you might do well to rid yourself of this lad. I know there's a big chance he might not pull through or be lame if he does. Now, I've got the time to nurse him to health. And I need a boy around the place. His being lame won't matter." He put his cup down and eyed her suspiciously.

"You don't expect me to give him to you, do you? What about my investment?" She could tell he was anxious to rid himself of the boy, but he was hoping for something in return.

"I'll give you one hundred dollars in gold money. That's all I have. Take it or leave it. That's all he's worth to me, considering the shape he's in. But I hope to make him well again," she added, know- ing full well the boy would be up and seen on the town's streets. "Still," she explained, hastily, "it will take some time and doing."

"Would you take care of him and let me pay you?" She had been expecting him to ask that.

"Well, I could. But there's room and board and the medicine and Doctor Murray's bills. He needs clothing, too." There, that ought to make him reconsider her offer. The stage was set for the clincher. "Wonder how long you'd get to work him after he re- covers? Mrs. Dorman told me she overheard the judge saying it won't be long before the slaves are freed in Texas, regardless of the outcome of the War." This was not a bold-faced lie. There had been talk of some sort or other of Texas honoring Lincoln's decree and freeing the slaves. It was not popular talk, however.

"If he was full-grown, I'd hire you to care for him. But, he's not too big at best. What with probably being lame, I don't aim to spend any more on him. But, Ma'am, he's a good boy, I'm sure," he added. "And he did work all right and earn his keep while I had him. Gold money, you say? One hundred dollars? What about Doc- tor Murray's bill today?"

Why, you penny-pinching Irishman, she thought. But she was pleased he was going to take her offer. She walked over to the cup- board and pulled out the jar with the money in it. Carefully she counted ten-dollar gold pieces, stacking them on the table. Just as carefully, Jordan felt and counted each one.

"I'll run over to the newspaper office and get the notary to make out the bill of sale." He pushed back his chair, leaving the money on the table. "Miz Banks, you sure you want to do this?"

His concern must not make me weaken. I've got to think about Muddy, she cautioned herself, silently. "Yes, Captain Jordan. I'm certain."

"Then put that money up until I return." He went to the door and pulled on his cap. "I hate taking a widow's last money."

"Don't be sentimental, Captain Jordan. This is a pure and simple business deal. It will give me something to do with my time." *Oh, what a lie that was. I have less time than anyone to waste on healing a sick boy,* she thought.

"But the doctor's bill?"

Bethel shrugged, "I'll trade him a cake or two."

Miz Banks placed her last pie for the hotel in the huge oven. She went into the living room to open the drapes and look down the road toward town. The road was empty. Would Captain Jordan come back with the bill of sale today? She wanted to move Muddy upstairs, but dared not, for fear of waking him. She tiptoed into the room and touched his forehead. He was still feverish. She hoped the captain had not seen through her plan. "Humph!" she snorted. President Lincoln had already freed Muddy, regardless of what the State of Texas said. Then she saw Captain Jordan, with the rolling gait of a sailor, hurrying toward her house. *Oh, dear,* she thought. *I hope he hasn't changed his mind.*

He banged on the front door of the house. She rushed to open it, not wanting the noise to awaken Muddy. "Come inside the house, Captain Jordan. You're just in time for hot peach pie and coffee."

"Can't, Miz Banks. Got to shove off. Word's come the block-ader's headed for Galveston. I just might be able to give her the slip. And that one hundred dollars will be right handy to have when we

put in at Veracruz." He strode around the neat living room, impatient to leave.

She nodded and went to the Seth Thomas clock on the wide mantel over the fireplace. Opening it, she revealed its contents. There were two vials of medicine for pain, laudanum and morphine; there was her husband's railroad watch; and the children's baby rings. And there were the ten gold pieces she had placed there for safekeeping after their conversation earlier that day.

Captain Jordan reached up under his dark wool jumper and drew out the bill of sale. He handed it to her and she read it quickly before handing him the money. She tried not to show her relief as she smiled up at him.

"Thank you, Captain Jordan. I hope I can get him back on his feet soon. I certainly need him around the place now that Sid and the boys are gone."

"If you can save him, you've got yourself a bargain. Good adult slaves cost a thousand dollars or more, nowadays, that is, if you can find one. Well, I'm going. Nice doing business with you, Ma'am." He turned and went out the door, not bothering to close it in his haste to get back to the docks and put out to sea.

Bethel realized his would not be the only ship trying to reach the open waters of the Gulf of Mexico. Couriers with fast horses were stationed along the channel and the Gulf Coast for just such an occasion. Each cotton factor in the vicinity would be trying to get his cotton out to Mexico. She closed the door and walked over to the big chair and sat down, exhausted. Too much excitement this day. Slowly she began to read each word of the bill of sale. She did not believe in owning slaves, but how else could she have rescued Muddy?

Miz Banks
bought Muddy to save
him

BILL OF SALE

State of Texas }
County of Jefferson }

Know all men by these presents, that I, Jackson Jordan of said State and County, in consideration of the sum of One Hundred Dollars to me in hand paid by Bethel Banks of said State and County, the receipt of which is hereby acknowledged, have bargained and sold and by these presents do sell and convey unto said Bethel Banks of Sabine City, a certain Negro slave named Boy and described as follows: Medium color, slight build, thirteen years old at best reckoning, able-bodied and no distinguishing marks.

And I bind myself and my executors and administrators, to warrant and defend the title to said slave, his heirs and assigns and to warrant the said slave at the time of sale sound in mind and body, and a slave for life. Witness my hand and scroll for seal the 5th day of March, 1863.

In the presence of: Sign: *Jackson Jordan*
C. M. Daniels   *Tom K. Schwing, Notary*
Hobie Roundtree   Jefferson County

It's like selling a piece of land, or a horse or a mule, not a real, live, breathing human being with a soul and a mind. Miz Banks hastily put the paper away, folding it to fit inside the back of the clock. She could hardly stand to touch it.

Chapter 7

WAS HE IN HEAVEN? He blinked his eyes twice, trying to focus. Everywhere he looked it was white and fluffy. He cautiously raised his head from the pillow to look around him. Then he realized he was in a white folks bed. Mosquito netting hung from the tester overhead, shutting out the rest of the room. He could see only shadows or shapes. He looked like a raisin in the center of a frosted cookie. The soft pillow and feather mattress bulged about his thin, black body. *What? Who?* Questions chased each other, knocking the cobwebs from his drugged mind. Yes, now he began to remember. The old woman and the doctor man gave him something bitter to drink. Who put him to bed? Why here, instead of the barn? What kind of people lived here in Sabine City? White people don't hide runaway negroes in their bedrooms.

His leg throbbed as the events of his escape paraded before his closed eyes. He sat up but dared not leave the bed. Where would he go? *Wonder where the old lady—what was her name—oh, Miz Banks—was?* And he remembered his new name—Muddy Boy Banks. She'd promised she would change it, but he had to think one up by himself. He crawled over to the edge of the bed and lifted the netting to peer out the nearest window. About dark, but what day? Was it still the same day he ran away?

Footsteps sounded on the stairs outside the opened door. He dropped the netting into place and pulled the quilt up over his chin. In his haste, he hurt his leg, and it was all he could do to keep from crying. He closed his eyes and pretended to be asleep. He'd listen if they talked, and then he'd make plans to leave. The woman was first to speak.

"Doctor Murray, he's still asleep. I'm worried about him."

And the man's voice answered. "You needn't be. He's awake, and just playing 'possum. See his toes wiggling under the quilt?"

Oh, those toes, thought Muddy, as he slowly opened his eyes and stared at the white man and woman holding up the net and leaning over him.

"Muddy, how do you feel? Does your head hurt? Is your leg paining you? Are you sick at your stomach?"

"Whoa, there, Bethel. Don't be giving him ideas. You've suggested enough ailments to keep this boy in bed for a month."

"Why, Doctor Murray, I meant—"

"Hush, woman. I'm short on time. I need to get home. Leave me and the boy for awhile. There's things to be done." Muddy watched the doctor shoo the woman back into the hall and close the door. He raised himself on his elbow so he could see better. Was the doctor mad at Miz Banks? What was going to happen, now? He remembered the doctor putting the salve on his leg. Now what? Muddy slid way down in the bed again, waiting.

Doctor Murray turned back the covers and began gently to unwrap the bandage from around Muddy's leg. "Far too much cloth on this, but it served our purpose." Muddy did not understand. He tried not to cringe as the doctor examined his wound. "Muddy," said Doctor Murray, his voice solemn, "you're one lucky black boy. You know that, don't you?" Muddy did not answer. He was trying to understand the doctor's statement. "If anyone else had found you, you'd be on Captain Jordan's steamer headed for Veracruz right now. By tomorrow, you'd probably have blood poisoning, and by the end of the week you'd be dead. You understand?" He gave Muddy's shoulder a slight shake, for emphasis. Muddy nodded, although he did not understand. Doctor Murray seemed satisfied with him, though, and continued speaking. "Miz Banks used all her money to buy you from Jordan. She wanted to keep you and make you well. She'll give you a good home and take care of you. Do you hear me, boy?"

The doctor's voice was stern, for Muddy had closed his eyes and had sunk back into the pillow, pulling the cover up over his face.

"I said, 'Do you hear me, Muddy?'" Doctor Murray jerked the cover back. "Are you going to answer me or not?"

"Yassuh."

"Yes, sir, what?" The doctor pulled Muddy by his shirt into a sitting position.

"I hears you."

"What did I say?"

"I've been bought again. I ain't free." Tears of self-pity slid down the young boy's face. "I'll never be free." He turned his face from the doctor, ashamed of his tears.

Muddy's despair seemed to affect the doctor more than his wound had. He turned to leave the room, then seemed to think better of it. He walked to the foot of Muddy's bed and stood waiting for Muddy to stop crying. Finally, as the boy made an effort to control himself, the doctor began to speak.

"Muddy, don't cover your face. You look at me." Muddy obediently removed the tear-dampened sheet from his face and gazed sullenly at the white man. "Son, I don't know what to tell you. I reckon I do sympathize with you, for no one wants to be *owned*." He ignored Muddy's snort of derision. "But your situation must be considered as it is. You are a slave. But you have the choice of two masters. First, you had Boss Jordan, and you ran away. Then along comes a soft-headed widow woman who used all her savings to buy you. She takes you in like you were one of her own kin and offers to nurse you back to health. Now, hear me well, Muddy Banks. You can stay here until your leg is healed, and then be returned to Boss Jordan. Or," he shook his finger at Muddy, "you can stay here and be grateful and help Miz Banks. Which will it be?"

Well, thought Muddy, *at least I get a choice for the first time in my life.* He delayed giving his answer as long as he could, still resentful of the white people and their opinions concerning slavery. But he was smart enough to know not to push the doctor too far. He said, with a don't-much-care tone to his voice, "I'll stay here."

"Mind you, Muddy, if you do one thing to give Miz Banks trouble, you'll answer to me and some of the other men in this town. Is that clear?" This hinted threat of punishment produced a respectful response from the black boy.

"Yes, sir. I'll treat Miz Banks fair." *But I won't like it,* he promised himself. *When I get a little bigger and my leg is all right, I'll show them. I won't stay here in Sabine City, Texas the rest of my life as a slave to an old widow woman witch,* he vowed silently.

"Good," said Doctor Murray, not knowing the boy's thoughts, hearing only his promise to be good. "Now I've got to go. Bethel," he called, opening the door. "Bring up some hot water and fresh bandages. I've got to open this cut and let it drain."

Chapter 8

MUDDY stayed in bed for three days with his throbbing leg propped up on pillows. Four times each day the widow would bring her big black kettle of hot water and an armload of towels upstairs. She would wrap his leg in the towels soaked in hot water. As soon as each towel cooled, she would re-soak it in hot water. Muddy hollered the first time, but gradually got used to the hot packs. "If the water doesn't burn my hands, Muddy, I know it's not burning your leg. I think you are a sissy," she teased.

Well, decided Muddy, *you mean old white lady, you aren't going to call me a sissy any more.* But he did not say it out loud. He gritted his teeth and endured the treatments. He had to admit, after he got used to it, that the water was not too hot.

Muddy was not permitted to suffer in peace. *No, sir,* he thought. *She can't stand a body just plain resting.* For on the second day, Bethel had caught him looking at one of Jed's old school books. He had been sounding out the words the best he could and had not heard her enter the room.

"Muddy, your fever's gone," she announced. "I know, however, you are still uncomfortable, and cannot put any weight on your foot. But," her face was stern, and her voice registered no sympathy, "I won't permit you to waste valuable time sitting up here fretting about your bad luck. If you stay under my roof, you are going to learn to read and write."

His eyes dropped before the determination in hers. His instinct to survive cautioned him to keep silent and not let her know he was able to read a little and write his numbers. He faked a frown so she could not detect how happy her threat made him. She might think he was trying to be uppity, as his former owners had declared when he had asked permission to study with Young Massa Richard.

46

They had refused. The tutor would send him back to the kitchen when it was time for Young Massa's lessons. Muddy had managed, with Young Massa's help, to hide in the closet during some of the first sessions. But Young Massa soon wearied of that game and told on him. Muddy stared at Miz Banks, his lip protruding in a pout. *Why didn't she ask him if he would like to learn to read and write? Why did white folks always think black people wanted to be dumb? Why couldn't she say, "Muddy, I'd be pleased if you would let me learn you how to read and write." No,* he thought, *she tells me what I've got to do.*

But his thirst for learning overcame his hurt pride. He mumbled a curt "Yes'm" to the woman at the foot of his bed holding the stack of school books.

"What did you say, Muddy?" she snapped at him, quick as a flash.

"Yes'm," he mumbled once more.

"I'm not going to waste my valuable time teaching a boy who mumbles and hasn't got enough gumption to speak up!"

"Whee!" gulped the surprised Muddy, the wind of resistance leaving his lungs. *She means every word, too,* he decided, pulling in his bottom lip and straightening up in the bed. *She's certainly different from any white folks I ever knew. Most times they want black folks to keep their mouths shut.* He licked his lips as he shaped the words he thought she wanted him to say.

"Yes, Ma'am. Thank you, Ma'am. I'll try hard," he said. And he meant it. He intended to watch his step. He was not going back to Boss Jordan. And he was going to read and write, just like Young Massa Richard. He was going to show her he could be as smart as any white boy—smarter. They would see.

Miz Banks came up twice a day to give him lessons. While she was busy baking or tending the stock, he worked on his assignments. And he tried to stay ahead of her teaching. He did not know how long the lessons would last. When the time came for him to run away again, it would be easier for him if he could read and write. He did not tell her he was studying in the other books kept in the sea chest at the foot of the bed. He let her think she was making him study. It was safer that way.

The spelling lessons gave him the most trouble. "It's because you are used to saying the words incorrectly," she had said when he had wanted to give up on the word list she gave him one day.

"But that's the way I heard Massa Richard say it," he had complained.

"Yes, I'm certain he spoke that way. But he was from Georgia, and had a distinct accent of his own. As I do, and you have an accent, too, Muddy." She grinned when she saw the look of distress on his face. Then her face softened. "Muddy, you are doing very well, and I'm proud of you," she said. "You are doing fine with your reading. You will soon be through your first primer."

He wanted to laugh at her statement, since she did not know he was already in McGuffey's third reader.

She was not finished with her lecture. "Muddy, I can give you food and clothes. I can help you grow well and strong. But I can't make you learn. I can only try."

Muddy gazed out the window trying to seem unconcerned. *You old witch*, he thought, *you won't have to make me learn. I'm going to know everything before I leave this house.* He still referred to her as "old witch" in his mind, even though his resolve to hate all white folks was gradually weakening.

By the end of the week he was permitted to go down the stairs. The day soon came when Miz Banks told him to clean the kitchen while she worked outside tending the stock. "This is woman's work," he had complained the first time she told him to do the dishes.

"Yes, kitchen work is mostly woman's work. Yet feeding and watering the stock, and killing and dressing all that poultry, is man's work. When you're able, Muddy, we'll look at our working arrangements. Perhaps we can come up with more manly chores for you, and womanly chores for me."

She cocked her head over to one side, as though waiting for his consent. She was fair, he knew. She never gave an unnecessary order or forced him to do anything he felt was demeaning. He saw she was still waiting in the doorway for his answer.

"Miz Banks, do I have to do the churning?" Young Massa Richard had teased him about having to churn for his mammy at Green Gates. He had hated it.

"No, Muddy. I'll churn this afternoon while you read to me from your reader." *Trapped again*, Muddy thought disgustedly.

"Miz Banks, aren't you ever going to let me go outside and look around? You promised it wouldn't be long."

"I know. Doctor Murray told me this morning all danger of reinjury would be past by Monday." Muddy could hardly wait. He wanted to explore the docks down below the house. From his bedroom window he could see a fisherman's shack near the docks. There was a white boy about his age staying there some of the time. *But, I'm not interested in knowing a white boy, never*, he vowed.

The creaking of the winches aboard the docking *Petit Ami* woke him from his daydream. "It's in," he whispered in his delight. And what a catch, he thought. Even from a distance he could see

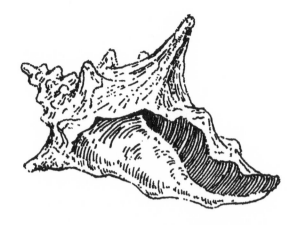

that the shrimp boat's hold teemed with the squirming shrimp and small fish. *I've got to go down to that dock today,* Muddy vowed silently. He leaned out the open window as far as he could. He did not hear the soft footsteps as Bethel slipped up behind him and yanked him back into the room.

"Muddy Banks, are you trying to break your neck?" She looked down at him, her hands on her hips, her eyes blazing.

"No, Ma'am. I was trying to see the shrimp boat. See," he gestured, "it's back."

"I never saw a shrimp boat so full of shrimp in my whole life," was her comment.

Sensing she was sympathetic, he pleaded, his eyes wide with expectation, "Please can I go up close?"

"It's only Saturday, Muddy."

"I know, but I'll be careful. It's not like I was going to be running and playing. Just looking, Miz Banks."

"All right, Muddy. You may go. Do you think you can buy some shrimp for us if I give you the money?"

"Oh, yes, Ma'am. The best they got." He was tingling with excitement as he waited for his instructions and the money.

Muddy walked slowly toward the docks. The oyster shell hurt his feet. The soles of his feet were bare and tender from his being housebound for three weeks. And all that washing, he thought, wincing as his left foot hit the protruding sharp shell. He decided to skirt the road by walking on its grassy edge. He was determined to reach the dock. His face flushed as he heard two fishermen from a nearby boat laugh at his plight.

"Look, Simonet, see the first tenderfooted nigger you ever did see." But Muddy paid no attention to them. His mammy had taught him to ignore white folks' slurring remarks. He climbed the steps to the wharf, and there she lay, the *Petit Ami*. The young boy and the old man were loading the shrimp into baskets. The boy looked up and waved at Muddy. Muddy did not smile or return the greeting. He did not intend making friends with any more white boys. Young Massa Richard had cured him of that.

Muddy stood out of the way, watching the fishermen work. He was fascinated by the ease with which they handled their catch. Both the man and the boy never missed the baskets, either fish or shrimp. Their work was interrupted when two ladies from town came up on the dock. Muddy stepped back but remained close enough to hear their conversation. He listened as they bargained with the old man for the shrimp. Finally after much haggling, the old man and the women agreed on the price. *So,* he thought, *that's how it's done.* He had not told Miz Banks he had never shopped before. He watched closely as the old man weighed the shrimp.

"Five pounds, Madame. That will be fifty cents, please." A frown creased Muddy's forehead. Miz Banks had said to get only one pound but she had given him twenty cents. Would he be expected to haggle before he could get shrimp for the same price as the ladies had paid? He was determined to spend Miz Banks' money wisely. He stepped forward and spoke to the man.

"I want one pound of shrimp, please."

"Oh, you do? You got some money, yes?"

"Yes, sir. One pound of shrimp, please." Muddy felt uncomfortable under the squinting stare of the sailor.

"What's your name? First time you make a pass by here, no?"

The man spoke as the fishermen did in New Orleans, remembered Muddy.

"My name is Muddy. I belong to Miz Banks."

"Oh, that's so? Well, me, I'm Pete Placette. I know that fine lady, yes. So, I give you one big pound of the best shrimp in all Sabine Lake." He turned to the boy who had stopped lugging the baskets and was watching Muddy and the old man. "Hey, you lazy Jo Bear. Bring me some big boys. It's for Madame Banks. This *ti neg* her boy."

Again the boy waved a friendly greeting to Muddy. Muddy forgot and smiled. And he continued to grin as he listened to the man and the boy call to each other. Miz Banks would have her hands full in correcting their pronunciation, he thought. And they were white, too.

The boy called "Jo Bear" brought the shrimp up to the old man. Captain Placette weighed them, then placed them in the mesh bag Muddy had brought from the house. But Captain Placette laughed and refused the money Muddy held out to him. "You tell Madame Banks she's owing me nothing."

"She sent this money." Muddy did not understand.

"Tell her two dozen of her best croissants by tomorrow afternoon. We pass by for them."

"You don't want the money?"

"Croissants. She'll know. Now go. That Jo Bear wants to make you friends. We got no time for friends. Not today." Muddy, startled by the abruptness of Captain Placette's words, looked at Jo Bear. The French boy nodded and grinned.

"I make a pass by you house tis even." Muddy nodded, though he did not understand. He had heard the words; he had recognized the words; but he did not know what the boy meant by them. He turned and left the wharf to begin his slow and torturous return trip over the shell road.

Bethel was standing at her front door when he arrived. He proudly showed her the shrimp. Water from them was still dripping through the mesh bag. She came out into the yard where he was standing.

"That's too many, Muddy. I didn't give you that much money."

He held out his hand and showed her the coins she had given him. "They said 'No money' for the shrimp."

"Was Captain Pete the man you talked to?"

"I reckon. He said, 'Me, Pete Placette.'"

"The old booger. I'll bet he wanted something besides money. What was it?"

Muddy thought for a moment. Could he say it like the sailor had? "Craw sunts. Two dozen tomorrow afternoon."

"Croissants, Muddy. That's a French word for a crescent or quarter-moon shaped roll with nuts and sugar on it. Here, let me have that bag. We'll take them out back to clean. Did you ever clean shrimp, Muddy?" They walked to the backyard where Muddy sat on the back steps. He was glad to be off his still-sensitive leg.

"No'm. Don't ever remember eating any either."

"Well, you'll like them. Here, let me show you how to clean them." She showed him how to snap the shell from the shrimp. Then she deveined them by running a tine of a table fork up the back of each shrimp, opening it. She showed Muddy how to flush the opening clean in a bucket of water. Muddy watched awhile before helping. He did not like the feel or the smell of them.

After awhile, he looked up from his work and slyly asked, "Woman's work?"

"No, man's work." She laughed at his look of disgust. "Shrimp and fish and wild turkeys and ducks and deer and doves are to be cleaned by the man who brings them into the house. They're wild. If I raise it, I clean it. See?" He did not see but he accepted this new rule, for she had been fair in all the other rules she had made. He knew it was about time for them to consider man's work and woman's work. He knew he was able to do some of the outside work, even now. He watched with interest as she showed him how to dispose of the shells.

She used a spade from the section house. He offered to dig the hole. "No, I'll do it. I'm afraid you might pull on your wound." "Why don't we throw them to the chickens?"

"I'd rather bury them. Even if the chickens did finally eat them all, there's still the smell until they are all gone." She covered the ill-smelling shells with the last spadeful of dirt. While she was patting the dirt down, he asked a question that had been on his mind since leaving the dock.

"Miz Banks, what does 'make a pass by you house tis even' mean?"

"Who said that?"

"That white boy off the boat."

"Jo Bear?"

"That's what it sounded like. Jo Bear."

"Now, that's nice. You could use a friend. Jo Bear and Captain Placette are from South Louisiana. Come inside and I'll show you where that is on the map." They went inside and she set the bowl of cleaned shrimp on the cabinet. "Now, Muddy, let me pour some vinegar in a small bowl and we'll wash the smell of the shrimp from our hands." Muddy did as she suggested, but he almost preferred the smell of shrimp to the smell of the vinegar. Then she led him into the living room, where she pulled the large geography book from the bookcase. Muddy had never seen this book. She turned to a page with lines and writings and a drawing he did not understand. For the next thirty minutes she explained about maps and the location of Texas and Louisiana on the Gulf of Mexico. She even showed him Georgia. It was easy for him to understand. She pointed to Galveston. He saw the words "Sabine Pass."

"Don't worry, Muddy. We will study it again. Now, sit in the kitchen while I tell you why Jo Bear and Captain Pete speak as they do." Muddy still did not know what the other boy had told him.

"Miz Banks, what did he mean?"

"Oh, Muddy. I'm sorry. He said he was going to come by our house this afternoon after work and visit."

"He's coming to see you?"

"Well, yes, in a way. I know Jo Bear. But I imagine he's mainly coming to see you." Muddy sat down in the rocker by the stove and slowly rocked, deep in thought. A white boy his own age was coming to see him? Maybe to be a friend? Finally he looked over at the widow, who had been watching him.

"What will we do?"

"Well, talk if you can. Maybe Jo Bear will tell you how it is to work on a shrimp boat. Don't worry, Muddy. That Jo Bear never knows when to shut up. Your problem will be trying to understand him." She sat down beside Muddy and began to explain. She related in detail the story of the exiled Acadians who were forced to leave their homes in Canada. She had him fetch the mapbook from the living room.

Turning to another section of the book, she showed him the map of Canada and traced the Acadians' long and perilous journey to Louisiana. "These were French people. They brought a different dialect to Louisiana. And after mingling with the people who spoke true French, and those who spoke English as we do, they developed their own way of speaking. We call it Cajun." She waited for Muddy to absorb this information. "Jo Bear and Captain Pete speak Cajun now. The Cajuns mostly have had little education and contact with other people. The way they throw their words together sometimes makes little sense to other people. But," she placed her hand on his shoulder before he could interrupt her, "Muddy, remember the way most of the field hands talk back in Georgia?" He nodded. "It's hard for many white people to understand them, too."

"Miz Banks, I understand you most of the time, if you don't go too fast."

"Yes, you're trying very hard. Do you now see why it's important for a person who's going to make this country his home to learn to speak its language?"

"Yes'm. Yes, Ma'am!" Muddy grinned broadly as he corrected himself.

"Get your slate. Before Jo Bear gets here, I want to explain about his name." Bethel wrote "Jo Bear" in large letters on the slate. Muddy spelled it out. Then he wrote it several times. "Now, Muddy, that's what his name sounds like. This," she quickly erased the lettering on the slate, "is the way it should be spelled. It's a French name." She printed "Joubert" on the slate. "If it were an English name, we'd say Joo-burt. But in French, it's called Jo Bear."

"Which way do I print it, if I want to write his name?"

"Jo Bear. Someone taught him to sign his name that way. And Muddy, he doesn't read and write anything but his name. You must never embarrass him."

"He's white. How come—"

"Many white boys and girls have had no schooling. And in South Louisiana, there are no schools along the bayous where Jo Bear lived."

"Oh." This was a new bit of information he would have to think about when he had time. Funny, being free did not mean you could do everything.

Chapter 9

MUDDY sat on the bench under the chinaberry tree. He had been waiting at least fifteen minutes. How proud he was that he could now tell time. He had worried the widow until she had spent one whole afternoon teaching him. He had never realized how important time was until coming to live with her. She went by the clock in baking. She went by the clock in teaching him. And they depended on the alarm of the clock for getting up, especially on rainy mornings.

He had worked for the printer delivering circulars and had earned enough money for the second-hand pocket watch he clutched in his hand. Jo Bear had promised to meet him at ten o'clock sharp. Miz Banks had said he could go with Jo Bear to set some traps and run Jo Bear's trotline.

Jo Bear had become his friend. He was glad, for Jo Bear laughed a lot, especially when he knew Muddy was having a hard time understanding his Cajun talk. One day Muddy asked Bethel why she did not tell Jo Bear when he wasn't speaking correctly.

"Muddy, it's not polite to correct other people's speech."

"You correct mine." He was not sullen, only curious.

She seemed to understand. "Why, it's different with you. You're family. I'm responsible for you. Jo Bear's a guest."

"If Jo Bear wanted to learn how to read and write, would you teach him? Would you correct him as you do me?"

"Yes. If he asks me to help him, I would do what I could. But not until he asks me. You have to be careful about things like that. Some people resent your offering help."

"Oh."

"Why? Has he said something about learning to you?"

"No, Ma'am. I jes—I just was thinking on it."

"Thinking about it."

"Yes, Ma'am. I was just thinking about it." Again this morning, he was thinking about Jo Bear who couldn't read or write. He wondered what Jo Bear would say if he volunteered Miz Banks' help. It would be fun to study the *Texas Almanac* and Mr. Webster's dictionary together. He had finished the primers and the readers. Sometime he would try reading the Bible, but Miz Banks said he was having a hard enough time with the way she spoke, much less having to struggle over the "thees" and "thous." She read the Bible to him every night. When she caught him humming and singing some of the tunes his mammy had sung, she would show him in the Bible the story that had inspired the words.

Muddy moved to the back porch where he sat swinging his legs impatiently. *That Jo Bear. Didn't he know he was supposed to be on time? He needed to hear Miz Banks' lecture on the "Precious Grains of Sand."* Then Muddy heard the cheery whistling coming down the road. He ran around to the front of the house. Sure enough, there was Jo Bear carrying his bundle of bait in one hand and a musket over his shoulder. *A gun? Captain Pete let Jo Bear have a gun?*

He knew Jo Bear was an orphan when Captain Pete took him in after the yellow fever swept through Texas and Louisiana. Captain Pete let Jo Bear do anything he wanted to, as long as Jo Bear was ready when the *Petit Ami* was due to leave the dock. Some days Jo Bear went pole fishing, and some days he would run his traps or trotline. Mostly he just sat around and ate and slept or visited with the Irish soldiers at the fort. Nobody bossed Jo Bear, except when he worked on the shrimp boat.

"Hey, there, Jo Bear. How come you're so late?"

"Huh, me? I've been down to the fort. Them Irishmen sure can do some work." Muddy was beginning to understand almost everything the Cajun boy said.

"Will you take me down there someday?"

"You ain't been there yet? How come?"

"I'm a slave. You know that."

"So, Miz Banks don't care nohow where you go. She done say so."

"I know. As long as I keep my chores done and my bookwork done, I can go. It's because I don't like those men. They'll fight to keep me a slave."

"Those men at the fort'll fight to keep you a slave? No, Muddy. Those men fight to keep them Yanks from eating us alive. Don't you know? Yanks are devils!"

"Miz Banks is a Yank. She ain't a devil, you crazy Cajun!"

"A Yank? Is she?" The French boy's eyes widened and he set his musket and bundle on the ground as though to free his hands for clearer thinking. "She is? Bet Captain Pete he don't know that."

"He does so. I heered—I mean I heard them talking once about her pappy and his ship when she lived up north."

"Well, if she suits the captain, I guess I'll not fret me none about her being a Yank."

Muddy had had enough of talk. "Are we going to run your traps like you promised, or is it too late? You're shore pokey."

"Then pick up them flat feet, and let's get out of here." Jo Bear began to run toward the dock with Muddy at his heels.

Until today, Muddy had refused to ride in Jo Bear's pirogue. The dugout canoe appeared awkward and unsafe. Muddy was still haunted by the memories of his escape from the awful mud that had seemed to reach up and grab his feet and legs. But he had a strong reason now to risk the pirogue. He had to make a map of the area to guide him when he set out for freedom. He would run the trotline and traps with Jo Bear, for they would head in the direction of Taylor's Bayou and the way to Beaumont.

After they were settled in the pirogue, there was a brief delay. Muddy had to be taught how to paddle.

"No! No! *Mais*, no!" shouted Jo Bear as the pirogue circled and circled. After several attempts, they succeeded in moving forward. When they were well into the proper cadence, Muddy began to complain.

"You don't have to yell at me. I ain't deaf."

"No, but you're sure dumb about paddling."

"Maybe so, but I can drive a buggy. Can you?" The boys continued to paddle as they entertained themselves by reciting their merits and demerits.

As soon as the shoreline obscured the docks and the Banks' house, Muddy called a halt to their progress.

"We ain't there, yet," objected Jo Bear.

"I know, but I have to mark my map." He hoped Jo Bear would not ask questions. He hoped in vain.

The agile Cajun set the pirogue to rocking as he scrambled close to watch Muddy place landmarks on his map. "Why do you need a map? You ain't going nowhere."

He ignored Jo Bear's question. "How far is it to Taylor's Bayou by land?"

Jo Bear did not answer. Muddy raised his eyes to see why Jo Bear had not answered. Jo Bear always had an answer. "Jo Bear—" he began.

Jo Bear grabbed at Muddy's shirt front and twisted it in his fist. His faced whitened and each freckle seemingly enlarged and darkened. "You planning to run off, ain't you?"

Muddy refused to look at Jo Bear. "I've got to," he answered in a quiet but determined voice. "I've got to be free, Jo Bear. I've just got to be," he pleaded. "I promised my mammy."

"When you going?" Jo Bear exhaled and waited.

"Soon. I've got my 'needs' all ready. But I have to study me some more about the shortest way to Mexico."

"Mexico!" screamed Jo Bear. He took his paddle and smacked it against the water. "Mexico! You're daft! How are you gonna talk to all those foreigners down there? Even me, Jo Bear Prejean, I stay on the *Petit Ami* when we dock at Tampico." He released the oar and once more grabbed Muddy's shirt front. "Aw, *mais* no, Muddy. No, no, no! I ain't gonna let you. I'll tell—"

Muddy wrenched loose from his friend's grip and gave him a shove, sending Jo Bear flat on his back. "Then I'll run away when we get home. Miz Banks is helping Doctor Murray." He picked up his paddle and attempted to turn the pirogue toward Sabine City. Jo Bear counteracted his move with his own paddle.

When the boat stopped, Jo Bear begged, "If I don't tell, will you wait awhile?" Muddy rested his paddle across his knees and stared out across the marshland for a few moments. "Please, Muddy?"

"Promise in blood not to tell?" He reached for his pocket knife.

"Sure." Jo Bear stuck out his finger and both boys mixed their blood. Muddy did not tell Joe Bear he would have to leave by the middle of September before the nights got cold.

As they moved toward the first set of traps, Muddy mentally inventoried his "needs" hidden in the attic of the section house. He had sneaked Jed's outgrown clothing from the cedar chest. His cache included a coat, boots, an extra shirt, and a pair of trousers. An old sugar sack held several tins of food he had slipped from the pantry. He had pulled the worn blanket from between the mattress and springs of his bed. Miz Banks had placed it there to keep the rust from damaging the mattress. He hoped it would be spring before she decided to turn the mattress. His fingers caressed his pocket watch and then fingered his knife. *Yes, I've got my "needs." And my map.* Unlike his first abortive attempt to escape, he had provisions and a plan. He was ready but he could not understand why the thought of leaving Sabine City filled his chest with hurt, not joy.

Later that evening Jo Bear's whistle brought Muddy to the back porch. Jo Bear held a squirming baby alligator in his hands. "Me, I captured him in my throw net. I got no place to keep him, so you keep him." He thrust the alligator into Muddy's hands before he could object.

Muddy realized Jo Bear was waiting for his reaction, for he recognized the devilish glint in his buddy's eyes. If the alligator had been slimy like he thought all alligators were, he would have flung the animal into Jo Bear's face.

Instead he jumped from the porch and placed the alligator in the empty black pot used for boiling clothes. "Thanks, Jo Bear. I

Conflicting feelings about leaving

needed me a pet. I'll make him a cage tomorrow." He laughed as his disappointed buddy turned and ran back toward the dock. He had shown Jo Bear he wasn't afraid of the baby alligator. But he wasn't too happy, for he had suddenly realized animals were like people, either captured or free.

Several days later Muddy was upstairs supposedly studying his books. What he was studying was the map he was making to use in his escape. He had faithfully marked the route to Taylor's Bayou when he and Jo Bear had run the traps. He knew he would have to find the road to Beaumont before he could head south to Mexico. It would've been much easier for him to float down the Sabine River to the Gulf and follow the shoreline to Mexico. Or so he had thought until he had talked with his friend.

"But, no!" Jo Bear had warned. "Sometimes the sea is so rough even the captain get sick on our way to Tampico. No, Muddy, a little fishing boat would not do it."

Perhaps there was a shortcut through the marshes without having to go to Beaumont. Muddy sighed. If there were a hill or a mountain that he could stand on to see the coast and the land on the other side of Taylor's Bayou, then he could be more certain of his escape route.

"The lighthouse, would it do?" Jo Bear had asked.

"Could we go there in your pirogue? Is the river too swift out in the channel?"

"Me, I go there many times. I run me some traps over there, too. We could go if Miz Banks she don't care."

The pirogue still wasn't Muddy's idea of a safe way to travel, yet it was all they had. He scowled as Jo Bear called out, "Move on back. I'll push off and then jump in quick." Muddy climbed over the bundles of bait and the musket to the stern of the boat. He hoped there would be no trouble on this trip. Miz Banks knew he was going trapping, but she did not know they were going to the lighthouse. He clung to the sides as Jo Bear gave a big push to the boat and hopped in, nimble as a grasshopper.

"Take the paddle, Muddy. We've got to pole it out of here." The boys maneuvered the pirogue out from the beach. They skirted the oyster reef separating the two channels. Muddy pointed toward the area where he had jumped from the *Hamilton*.

"You some lucky boy, you. Supposing an old alligator done got you, huh? My papa killed himself one ten feet long, I betcha, when I stayed to home. My mama she scraped it and dried it and hung it over the fireplace. And man, we ate them alligator some much." Muddy laughed at his friend as he tried to understand what he was talking about. Maybe today he would ask Jo Bear if he would like to study with him.

They beached the pirogue near the base of the abandoned lighthouse. Jo Bear explained how it had been before the War when the lighthouse lamp burned faithfully each night.

"Why isn't it working now?"

"You don't know? You learning to read and write and me, Jo Bear Prejean, knows everything already." He shook his head in disgust. "You want that light to brang them Yankee devils through the Pass when it's dark?" The boys were so busy talking they failed to notice the incoming tide as they ran up the circular staircase to the top of the lighthouse. Jo Bear showed Muddy how to get out on the balcony that circled the big light. Muddy clung to the railing. His cheeks were flushed from the climbing and his heart was pounding with the excitement of being able to see for miles in all directions. It was higher than he had ever climbed in his life. To the south, the waters of the Gulf of Mexico stretched to the horizon. Over to the west, sandy beaches curved inland in a wide arc. Muddy pointed to the southwest.

"Jo Bear, look. That's where Bolivar and Galveston are."

"How come you know that? You ain't never been there."

"Miz Banks showed them to me on her big map. See, I copied them on my map." He dropped to his knees and pulled his map from his pocket.

"How about the Calcasieu? Where do it read that?"

This was the first time since making friends with Jo Bear that Muddy could do something better than the French boy. He had been right to study hard. Reading and writing did make a difference. He noticed new respect for him in the eyes of his buddy.

When they tired of studying the map and their surroundings, they decided to run the traps. They raced down the steep steps and out to the beached pirogue by the lighthouse. The victor of the race turned to the loser, crying, "Holy saints! Someone done stolen me pirogue!"

"Who would do that? There's no one here but us."

"A thieving Injun done took it, I betcha."

"Miz Banks said there ain't no Indians around here. Your boat floated off by itself." The boys started down the beach, searching behind the tall grasses.

"There she is. I see her!" Muddy caught up with him at the water's edge.

"Where? I don't—"

"See? Over past that big clump of reeds. I'm going to get her." He waded into the water and sank knee-deep in the mud.

"Come back! You'll drown in the mud!" screamed Muddy in remembered terror. "Come back!" His stomach churned at the thought of snakes lurking in the reeds and his own struggle through the mud.

"No. I've got to get her. She done belong to my papa and now she belongs to me." Muddy waited, hardly breathing as his friend moved through the submerged flat. Why, he'd die and rot on shore before he'd go out in that mud. Then Jo Bear disappeared behind a clump of tall reeds.

"Jo Bear! Can you hear me? Jo Bear!" When his buddy did not answer, Muddy raced up the steps to the lighthouse. At the top, he leaned over the railing searching for his friend. He located him north of the lighthouse. He began calling to him. Jo Bear finally saw him and signalled him to come out and help with the pirogue. He was struggling to bring the unwieldy dugout about. Several times Muddy saw the boat almost tip over as Jo Bear tried to climb inside. *He can't handle it by himself. I've got to help him. But all that mud?* Then he saw the shell-bottom approach they'd used coming to the lighthouse. It was narrow, only extending several yards into the channel. *I could go out that way and then swim up the channel to where Jo Bear is. I wouldn't even have to wade through all that mud like Jo Bear.* As he raced down the steps he made certain his pocket was buttoned. He didn't want to lose his knife. He knew he could make another map. He had to help Jo Bear. "I'm coming!" he yelled to his friend.

He stopped at the edge of the water. Memories of his escape from the *Hamilton* flooded his mind. Why should he help save that old boat? *Why should I help any old white boy? A white boy told a dirty lie about me and I got sold.* He weighed his fear of having to enter the water against his friendship for Jo Bear. *But Jo Bear can't help it if he's white.* Muddy put his fear behind him and waded out into the water. There were ripples on the water and the wind had come up. Small whitecaps dipped and bobbed out in the center of the channel. Already the oyster reef that separated the Louisiana channel from the Texas channel had disappeared under the tidal waters.

He gazed toward the grassy finger shielding Jo Bear and the pirogue from his line of vision. What if they lost the boat? They could make another. But he knew it would not be the same. This was Papa Prejean's handiwork. Would the current be as swift? Not daring to think any longer about the hazards, he plunged into the water and began swimming with the tide.

The salty water stung his eyes, but he was soon used to it. He didn't dare pause and tread water since there might be an undertow. He had to swim hard to cut across the main tidestream. Soon he was behind the grassy knoll treading water and grinning at the surprised Jo Bear who was about a dozen yards from the deeper water.

"Hey, Muddy, come on. You can stand up here."

"In the mud?"

"Ain't gonna hurt you none. You scared or something?"

"I don't like it."

"A little old mud's gonna keep you treading water all day long by yourself?"

"If you're in the mud, why can't you heft yourself into the boat?"

"Can't by myself."

Muddy began to dog paddle until the water became too shallow. Slowly he moved through the mud until he reached Jo Bear's side. "What do we do now?"

"You get down here at this end and pull down with all your might."

"Why?"

"Don't ask questions. Do like I say. We got to put all our weight on the boat to see if she sit in the mud when we do. We may have to move out into the water more." They tried to free their bodies enough to pull down on the pirogue. "Nope. Not enough water. She take about a foot, loaded. Let's move out."

Muddy gingerly surrendered the safe place where he had been standing. "I'm biggest. You go first, Jo Bear. I'll steady the boat on this side and you can climb over the other side."

"Just so you mind the boat she don't tip over too far." After a few attempts, Jo Bear was in the boat. Muddy wasn't as agile as his friend. Time and time again he tried to throw himself into the rocking pirogue. Jo Bear, yelling instructions, was little help. He finally shut up and looked at his frustrated friend hanging onto the side of the boat. "I can't paddle it across with you hanging on it. What we gonna do?"

"Let's take it out in the water more where I can swim. Then

maybe I can get in." Jo Bear agreed. Soon Muddy's feet had cleared the grip of the mud. He could feel the pull of the current on the boat and his legs. He had worked his way back to the stern as he shoved the boat to deeper water. He began to raise himself out of the water and over the stern. Jo Bear leaned out over the bow to compensate for Muddy's weight. Then he was in. For a while the two boys just stared at each other with relief.

Finally Jo Bear yelled, "Grab a paddle! We be in the lake soon if we don't head back for the dock." It was hard work paddling against the current. Soon they noticed the Irishmen had stopped their work and were standing on the bank near the fort, yelling and whooping at the two boys paddling toward the Texas shore.

"Something wrong over there, Jo Bear?"

"Naw. They just funning with us." He cupped his ear with his hand in an effort to hear what the men were shouting. "They're betting on if we land above the fort or below it. See them passing the jug around? They're through for the day." He laughed and waved his hand at them. "They sure do have themselves a time."

"Will they be mad if we don't land in the right place? I'm scared of them."

"You're scared of your shadow. Those Davis Guards talk loud, and mind you, they do brawl a bit, but they like children. And they're nice to the ladies, too."

"Miz Banks says they are the strongest men she ever saw."

"Use to working the docks. Me, I seen them in Galveston. They do sling them bales of cotton."

"Why are they here now? Why don't they have regular soldiers?"

"Captain Pete say there ain't many regular soldiers around here, just the Guards. This bunch too rough for Galveston. Lieutenant Dowling brung them here. Come on, paddle hard." Jo Bear leaned over the bow, ready to throw the weighted line. Muddy ducked his head and would not look at the men waiting to catch their line. Jo Bear grinned at him over his shoulder. "Get that scared look off your face. They ain't gonna hurt you. They're on our side. They

ain't no bloody Billy Yanks. They're Johnny Rebs." Muddy was pet-
rified when a smiling Irishman called to him to grab his hand. He
was pulled on shore with a jerk that almost tore his arm off. One of
the men slapped him on the back before handing him a nickel.

"What for?" Surprised at his windfall, Muddy gazed up into
the blistered face of his huge benefactor.

"For docking her here. I won the pot." Muddy didn't understand what the man was saying. He'd never heard the Irishmen talk
and it was worse than trying to understand Jo Bear. He nodded
politely and moved close to Jo Bear who was laughing and talking
with the men.

One of the men rubbed Muddy's head and asked, "Where did
you find this boy? You slave running out of Louisiana?"

"No, he belongs to Miz Banks."

"This the one jumped the *Hamilton?*" Muddy understood
enough to duck his head. They were talking about him. Was it that
they didn't like him for jumping?

"Yep, that's him all right. Miz Banks bought him off Boss
Jordan."

"Well, glory be," said the soldier, grinning unabashedly. "I'd be
proud to be shaking the hand of a fellow shipjumper." The other
soldiers began laughing as they saw the frightened boy's hand en-
gulfed by the hand of the immigrant.

As soon as he was released, he edged over to Jo Bear. "Let's go.
I've got to get to the house. I've got evening chores to do." *And I
need to make a new map before I forget where things go. And I've got to
think about these men. They don't seem mean. An enemy should seem
mean.*

Chapter 10

"MUDDY, WAKE UP!" She was shaking his shoulder. It couldn't be time to get up. It seemed no time at all since he had fallen asleep. Rubbing his eyes, he sat up in bed, voicing his complaint. She stood by his bedside, fully clothed and holding the lighted lamp. "Miz Banks," he protested as he leaned over to look at his watch on the table beside his bed. His mouth fell open when he saw what time it was. Two o'clock in the morning!

"I know it's very early. But get dressed and come downstairs. There's an emergency. I need you." She closed the door behind her, leaving the lamp. Not knowing what to think, but positively impressed by the word *emergency*, Muddy slid out of bed. He stumbled over to the washstand to get ready. Soon he was dressed and downstairs.

"Doctor Murray!" He stopped at the kitchen doorway, startled to see his friend at the table. The doctor looked up at the surprised boy.

"Come in the kitchen and sit down. She's got breakfast ready for you, too." He went back to eating as though his appearance at the Banks' house at that time of morning was an everyday occurrence. Muddy slipped into his chair beside the doctor, his eyes raised to the widow. He knew he had not done anything wrong that week. Not unless his pet alligator had scared the old rooster again. But Doctor Murray would not come at this time of night or day just for that.

In answer to his unspoken question, Doctor Murray said, "Get that 'I didn't do anything' look off your face. Eat your grits before they cool." The doctor patted Muddy's shoulder. "There's nothing wrong here. The emergency is at the fishing camp on Taylor's Bayou.

Young Pete LeBlanc's wife is due to have her baby. We're expecting trouble in its birthing."

Miz Banks' face wore a troubled look. "The doctor needs me to help him. Do you think you can handle the roll baking for the hotel?"

"Certainly he can!"

"No, let him decide."

"Yes, Ma'am, I can, if the fire's going. I don't know much about that stove." Muddy lifted his head as he spoke. "Would you write down on the paper what time I'm supposed to do each thing?"

"Well put, Muddy. I knew I could count on you. But I wanted it to be your decision." She began to make notes on the tablet.

"Come on, Doctor Murray, I'm ready." She handed Muddy his instructions, picked up the ever-ready birthing basket, and placed it on her arm. Muddy laughed with the doctor as they both saw the basket. Then Doctor Murray began to tease her about it.

"See you got your bribery basket." It contained candy, cookies, and other treats for the family she would care for during the birthing of the baby.

"Now, Muddy," Bethel began to caution from her place on the buggy seat, "be careful you—" Then she stopped. He stared up at her, waiting for her to finish her instructions. Instead, she smiled at him, then turned to the doctor. "Let's go. He can handle everything." Muddy's chest filled with pride as he watched them drive down the road in the bright moonlight.

Back in the kitchen, everything seemed different. Today this was his kitchen. Today he could do as he pleased. Today was the first time she had left all the baking to him. Of course, he admitted, not all. For the dough was rising in the large crockery bowls covered with white cup towels. The stove was hot, the oven nearly ready. He poured a glass of milk. His eyes glimpsed the tablet with the schedule she had set for him.

The first entry was "2:30 a.m.—put rolls into pans." Wonder how long that would take, he thought, never having paid too much attention to time when they were baking. She had set the pace and he had worked along with her.

"Oh, there it is," he said aloud as he continued to study the schedule. "4:30 a.m.—put in oven." He knew he would have to allow some time for the second rising, too. He looked at the clock on the wall. It was time to begin! Hurriedly he cleared the breakfast dishes from the table. Then, just as she had done, he clamped the canvas cloth to the table. *Oh, me. Forgot my apron.* He shook his head in disgust. Already he was getting careless. He tied it on and scattered flour from the sifter onto the canvas. Then he took the first bowl of dough and dumped it on the table. He had never worked with such a big pile of dough. He floured his hands and began to punch and knead the dough. Eyeing the clock, he moved as fast as he could. He must knead and punch and lift it up and slap it down, separating and mixing it until it was the right texture. When the dough reached that stage, he began to roll portions of it. Next came the cutting and the shaping of the rolls.

Lard? Where was the lard she used to grease the pans? He swung around, scattering flour in every direction. *There, over by the flour barrel.* The clock ticked on while he greased each pan. Now he could put the rolls in and cover each pan with the clean cup towels.

The fire! Did he need to put more wood on it? He checked, but it was fine. He put the first pan of rolls on the cabinet to rise. *Fifteen minutes. It took fifteen minutes for the first pan of rolls. I'll have to hurry. There's four more pans to fill.* He was tempted to take less time kneading, but he remembered how important the kneading was. By the time he had finished the dough, he was on schedule.

How long should he let them rise? The answer was on the schedule. "4:30 a.m.——put in oven." *I've got an hour, then. I'll clean the kitchen while I wait.* This was the part he hated about the baking, but he knew someone had to do it. Today that someone was him.

He had fifteen more minutes to wait. He'd washed and put away the dishes and mixing bowls. Once more he glanced at the clock. He poured another cup of coffee and sat down at the table.

Finally the clock registered 4:30. Carefully he slid each pan into the oven. Wouldn't it be terrible if he dropped and ruined the rolls? He shuddered at the thought. As he worked, he would have been amazed if he had seen himself. His hands and his face were clean—their natural, chocolate color. But his hair and his clothing were not. Everywhere bits of dough and flour clung to him. The apron had helped some. But in his haste to stay on schedule, he had scattered flour everywhere. He stared at the messy kitchen floor. Then he remembered the floured canvas had to be put back in the drawer after being shaken over the flour bin to salvage the loose flour.

Removing the clamps from the canvas, he carefully brought the edges of the cloth together as he tried not to scatter any more flour. He carried it over to the flour barrel and tried to shake the excess flour from the canvas. He shook so vigorously the flour floated up and around him. He began to sneeze. He waved one hand in front of his face to clear the air. Then he folded the canvas and placed it in the drawer.

Next he tried to sweep the floor. He was able to get some of the flour out the back door, but mostly it rose in the air and fell again to the floor. The smell of rolls baking reminded him he was hungry.

He opened the oven door. It smelled good. Would they taste as good? Would Mrs. Dorman at the hotel be satisfied? Taking the thick padded pot holders, he removed the pans from the oven and placed them side by side on the table. Then he covered them with the clean cloths as he had seen Miz Banks do. Breathing a sigh of relief, he stepped back from the table to view his handiwork. There was no time for rejoicing. He heard the rumble of the approaching cart. Quickly he removed two rolls from the nearest pan and hid them in the cabinet. He would eat them as soon as the rest of the rolls were on their way to the hotel.

Moses knocked at the back door as Muddy called, "Come in." He liked the old man.

"H'lo, young Muddy. How's ya'll this morning?"

"I'm fine, but Miz Banks, she ain't here. She's gone birthing with the doctor over Taylor Bayou way."

"But if'n she be gone, whomsoever baked them rolls?"

"I did."

"You?"

"Yes. Here, taste one." He handed a roll to the servant. Moses took the roll and slowly tested it. He swallowed the last bite and looked over at the waiting boy.

"Dat's good. They're real good. Now, hep me load them so I can get back to the hotel whilst they still be warm." Muddy felt like doing flip-flops but tried to act nonchalant and unimpressed with Moses' praise. He helped load the cart, being careful to tuck the edges of the towels around each pan. He was glad the hotel was not far away. The rolls would still be warm.

Returning to the kitchen, he reached for the two rolls he had placed in the cabinet. He couldn't wait until he fixed his ham and eggs. He bit into one after buttering it. Moses was right. It was good. Getting some milk to drink from the cooler reminded him he would have to do the milking and prepare the milk by himself. He was glad the widow had taught him how to do almost everything about the place. Not only would knowing those skills help him to-day, but he would also be able to find work when he ran away.

He consulted the list once more. There it was, "5:30 a.m.—set the dough to rising." He had watched her mix the dough, but he wondered if he could do it by himself. He set the kettle of water to boil. *Seems like there will be no end of dishwashing this day. I'll leave the milking until I get the dough ready. I don't know how long that will take me.* He opened the cabinet door and studied the recipe tacked to it. He could read every word. And he could follow those directions. He remembered the first time he read it aloud to the very surprised widow. He had a hard time concealing his pride.

He reached for the salt. *But first, I had better check the fire.* He opened the firebox and was relieved to see the fire was properly banked against the time of the next baking.

From under the table he pulled the big round shallow wooden dough pan. It was so large he couldn't reach his arms around it. He read the recipe once more. Now, the starter. He remembered the many times she had told him always to leave some starter for the next batch. He knew she couldn't make the next rolls without it. Into the dough pan went the left-over starter from the morning rolls.

The clock chimed the half-hour. It was the signal for him to hurry. He measured each ingredient. Soon he had a reasonable mass of dough piled high in the pan. He placed some of it in the starter box, for the next batch. Then he carefully divided the mass into equal amounts for the five big crocks he had greased. He covered these with towels. Again the clock chimed. He was on schedule.

Feeling justifiably proud, he leaned against the cabinet and grinned at the neatly covered bowls of dough. His feeling of accomplishment diminished as he gazed around the kitchen. Another big mess. *Flour everywhere. How does she keep things so tidy? She won't care if I don't clean up. That's woman's work.* His arms ached from working with the dough, but he knew he was going to clean the kitchen anyway. If she could do it, he could, too. He dragged his weary body from the cane-backed chair and stumbled toward the sink.

Suddenly there was a knock on the front door. *Lordy, who could it be? No one ever came to the front door.* He tugged at the latch. The knocking was louder and more insistent. *Oh, no. She didn't like my rolls.* For there stood the owner of the hotel, Mrs. Kate Dorman. Muddy stared, his face frightened.

"Well, may I come in?" *She doesn't sound angry, but why is she here?* Muddy held his breath as he opened the door and stepped back. "Cat got your tongue?" she asked.

"No, Ma'am. Miz Banks, she's not here," his voice squeaked.

"So Moses told me."

"You didn't like my rolls?"

"On the contrary. They were fine. But what about the dinner rolls? Will you be able to make them, too?"

"Yes, Ma'am. Please come into the kitchen. I'll show you."

She followed him into the kitchen and, to her credit, said nothing about the sprinkling of flour that covered everything, even the young baker.

"Here," he said, almost bursting with pride. He lifted the corner of one of the cloths on the bowls of dough. "The dough is ready and is starting to rise."

Mrs. Dorman inspected each bowl. Then she spotted the dough-smeared recipe on the cabinet door. "Have you ever made the rolls before?"

"No, Ma'am. Not by myself. But sometimes I help Miz Banks." Lines of worry creased the hotel owner's face. Muddy wondered what had suddenly upset her.

"Did you make the dough for the breakfast rolls?"

Oh, so that's it. "No'm. I only kneaded it, rolled it, and put them in the pans." Mrs. Dorman looked at the five crocks. She lifted the cloths on each one again. Then she shrugged.

"Well, Muddy, they'll have to do, I guess." Seeing his head drop at her statement, she smiled and placed her hand on his flour-covered shoulder. "But don't you fret. I reckon they'll be fine." She waved to him, then turned abruptly and sailed through the living room and out the front door. *Moves mighty fast for a lady.* He continued to watch from the front door as she hurried down the road. Miz Banks had said Mrs. Dorman was the busiest lady in all of Sabine City. He believed her.

He decided to wait until after he had filled the pans for the oven before cleaning the kitchen. Walking out on the back porch, he took off his apron and shook it. Again he covered himself with a cloud of flour. Between sneezes, he yelled at the cow. "Hush your bawling. I'm coming."

She gave him no trouble. Soon he had the cream in the churn and the milk in the cooler. His feet were dragging as he went to the section house for the chicken feed. He never realized how much there was to be done by one person. They had been sharing the chores since his leg had healed, but he had never been this tired. And he knew he would have to stay awake until he finished baking the dinner rolls. *I'll sleep all this afternoon.* After throwing the feed, he had to fill the water troughs. And there was Nell to feed and water, too.

At last, the stock was cared for, and he turned toward the coolness of the back porch. At the sound of a hen cackling, he stopped. *Eggs. I've got to gather and wash the eggs.* This was the morning he would have to get them ready for Lieutenant Dowling.

By eight o'clock he was hungry again. He fixed some ham and eggs and grits. He was almost through eating when he heard the sound of a shod horse coming toward the house. Gulping his milk

and pushing the last bite of ham into his mouth, he left the flour-covered table. As he was washing up at the pump outside, Lieutenant Dowling rode up.

The red-haired Irishman laughed out loud at the sight of the flour-covered negro boy. Muddy's underlip began to quiver. He didn't like doing business with the Davis Guards since they were in Sabine City to fight to keep him a slave. However he was finding it awfully difficult to dislike them. Yet here was their leader laughing at him. And he didn't know why. Lieutenant Dowling apparently realized Muddy didn't know how he looked to others. He stopped laughing and dismounted.

"I didn't mean to hurt your feelings. But you look like a ghost. Where's your mirror? Did you fall into a flour barrel?" Surprised, Muddy took a good look at his arms and clothes.

"Miz Banks done gone off with the doctor to a birthing. I'm doing the baking," he added sheepishly, with a wide grin.

"I hope the flour supply holds out. Have you got my eggs ready?"

"Yes, sir. They're ready." The lieutenant handed him his basket. Muddy began to count the eggs into it. The lieutenant watched closely and listened as the boy counted.

"You know your numbers, lad?"

Muddy kept counting without answering. Finally the required amount was in the basket. He closed the lid and lifted it to the man now on the horse. "Yes, sir. Miz Banks taught me my numbers and how to make change. I'm on adding and take-aways, now."

"Good. That way you won't get cheated."

"No, sir. 'Scuse me, sir. I'll get the signing paper." He did not know what the paper was called, but he knew each time the lieutenant or one of his men made a purchase, he signed for it. When he handed the paper to Lieutenant Dowling, he had already noted on it: "6 doz. eggs, Aug. 18, 1863," the date from the kitchen calendar.

"Very good. Now, can you have twenty fryers ready and dressed by three o'clock this afternoon?"

"This afternoon? This is Tuesday. Saturday's fryer day." Muddy's voice reflected his alarm. Twenty fryers to be caught, killed, and dressed by three o'clock? He didn't know if Miz Banks would be home by then.

"I know, lad. But General Magruder and his staff will be here for evening mess, and we want to feed them well. Can you manage it?" Though he had a look of sympathy on his face, his voice was firm. "I have to have them, and I can't spare any of my men to help you. We're trying to get the fort ready for inspection."

"If you have to have them, I guess I can get them ready." But Muddy did not feel as confident as he sounded.

"Good. Then I'll bring the wagon over at three this afternoon."

"Yes, sir." Muddy collapsed on the steps as he watched Lieutenant Dowling ride away. "Twenty fryers!" he moaned. "How can I do them by myself?"

Chapter 11

TWENTY FRYERS! *Why didn't Miz Banks come home? What time was it?* Dragging his feet, as though carrying a physical burden too heavy for his young shoulders, he trudged into the kitchen. His mind was blank as he stood in front of the clock on the wall. Eight forty-five! He had no time to think about the fryers. It was time to put the dinner rolls into the pans.

Once more he made preparation for rolling the dough which had been rising in the crockery bowls. No longer did the novelty of being in charge make preparing the rolls fun. Now it was work. He had lost his enthusiasm for baking and showing off his abilities. But he found it again as a lilting whistling sound signaled the approach of his Cajun buddy.

Jo Bear was coming! Muddy pounded the mass of dough in front of him with both fists. Jo Bear just had to help him. Weren't they friends?

"No, no, no, but no! Not Jo Bear Prejean." The French boy was lying on his back on the porch floor, his arms behind his head, his knees drawn up. Muddy stood over him, dressed in his flour-covered apron, reciting his woes.

"Please, Jo Bear. Miz Banks is counting on me to take care of things whilst she's gone."

"Counting on you, not me."

"But she's been good to you, too."

"Yes. But she's your people. You belong to her. Me, I belong to nobody. I'm going back to the *Petit Ami*. Maybe, I sleep me some." He raised himself to a sitting position, then paused, his eyes suddenly alert. "Twenty fryers, yes? Man, that do make some bait for my traps. You give me the guts, huh, Muddy?" He looked up with a wide grin of expectation on his face.

Muddy, so disappointed he could cry, turned away from Jo Bear. Even if his friend had let him down, he would still give him the guts. He almost said, "Sure," without thinking. It was Jo Bear's confident whistling that stopped him. Why should he give him anything? *I would have helped him. I know it will save me from having to bury the guts. But he shouldn't get them for free. Free—that's the answer. Jo Bear likes to trade.* Muddy turned around and tried to remain calm. "Jo Bear, I'll give you the guts to bait your traps if you'll help me." He stepped back as Jo Bear jumped to his feet.

"What do you mean, *help?*"

"Help me catch, kill, and dress those chickens. Hurry and give me your answer. I've got to get along with my baking."

"I'll catch them for you." Jo Bear's voice was wary.

"That's not enough." Muddy turned toward the kitchen door, his fingers crossed.

"Where're you going. I ain't said yet." He followed Muddy into the kitchen.

Trying to be casual, Muddy washed his hands at the sink as he said, "I've got to get the rolls ready." Still proud of his skill, Muddy took the flour sifter from the barrel and began to sprinkle flour on the canvas. Jo Bear stood close by, watching. *I'll bet he has never seen Miz Banks make the rolls.* With a flourish, he floured his hands and began to knead the dough.

Jo Bear began questioning him. Muddy explained why the kneading was so important, glad he could do so; usually it was Jo Bear who explained things to him.

"Is that the oven?" Jo Bear had been studying the kitchen.

"Yes." Taking a hot pad in hand, Muddy made a big show of checking on the fire.

"You know how to do that?"

"Sure. Now move out of the way. I've got to grease the pans." That task accomplished, Muddy began rolling the dough and cutting and shaping the rolls. By this time Jo Bear's fingers were twitching as his eyes followed each movement Muddy's hands made.

"Can I help? Please, Muddy. Let me help." Muddy knew there was enough room for them both to work at the table. *But wait, don't you be giving away any special privileges. Letting Jo Bear help would cinch the chicken business.*

"You gonna help me with them fryers?"

"Aw, why you gotta bring that up again for?"

"Is it a deal? You catch and kill them for the guts, and then you help me dress them for letting you make the rolls." He tried to keep his voice low and unconcerned. Would Jo Bear agree? Maybe he should add a bribe to help Jo Bear make up his mind. "If you hurry and decide, I'll make you a surprise."

"What kind of surprise?"

"A big old kolache surprise."

"Kolache? Me, I never heard of him, that kolache. What's that?"

"It's a big roll full of preserves with sugar and nuts on the top." *Miz Banks wouldn't mind if I made one for Jo Bear. Anything to get him to help.* "And I'll give you my dime, besides." There. That was all the money he had. He couldn't think of anything else to offer. He moved the pan of rolls over to the cabinet. After sprinkling more flour, he dumped the next crock of dough on the table and began to knead.

"So I'll do it. Where's my dough?"

Muddy grinned at his friend. Jo Bear's acceptance made the burden on his shoulders seem lighter. Jo Bear was a good friend. "Hold on, you crazy Cajun. You have to wash first. And take off that dirty shirt."

"Wash? I took me a swim in the lake this morning."

"Wash. And use the soap in the gourd. Wash up past your elbows, too. Then I'll give you one of Miz Banks' aprons." Grumbling all the while, Jo Bear washed his arms and hands and removed his shirt. Muddy tied the long apron under Jo Bear's armpits. Placing him on the far side of the table, Muddy handed him the sifter, then pointed to the bowl of dough he was to knead and make into rolls.

Jo Bear swung the sifter, scattering flour on his side as well as Muddy's. But Muddy knew better than to complain. He didn't want to lose his helper. In a few minutes, Jo Bear had calmed down and had begun to knead his dough. They worked, talking all the while. Muddy saved back some dough to use in making not one but four kolaches, two for him and two for his friend. The kolaches were large, and he heaped the filling on them. He placed them at the end of the last pan and set them back to rise.

As they washed up, Muddy outlined his plans for the fryers. "While the rolls are rising, I'm going to clean the kitchen and fix lunch. You go start the fire under the boiling pot and draw the water."

"I ain't bargained for no firemaking and water-drawing," the canny trader complained.

"You ain't bargained for no lunch, either. But I'm gonna make some, anyway. But I'll save myself some trouble if you think that firemaking and water-drawing is gonna kill you. Corpses don't eat lunch." The two boys eyed each other like banty roosters preparing to fight for control of the henhouse. Then Jo Bear threw up his hands in mock surrender.

"I'll do it. I'll do it. But, mind you, black boy, I'm hungry enough to eat a bear." Muddy began to whistle through his teeth as he cleaned the mess they had made. *Things are certainly going my way.* He would use the grits on the back of the stove, left over from his breakfast. Then he would get a ham from the smokehouse. They needed one in the kitchen, anyway. He looked in the cooler and saw there was milk and enough butter for the meal. At the sight of the butter he breathed a wish that Miz Banks would be back in time to do the churning. He knew yesterday's bread was wrapped in a damp cloth in the breadbox. Lunch was practically ready. He opened a jar of home-canned corn and set it simmering on the cookstove. *Now all I have to do is finish sweeping the floor.* He sighed with relief as he began to sweep the flour through the back door and off the porch. With Jo Bear's help promised for the chickens, he knew he could make the rest of the day, provided the wily Cajun kept his word.

Chapter 12

THE WIDOW always caught the chickens. She told Muddy she did it since she was afraid he might frighten the hens and cause them to quit laying. But poor egg production was the least of Muddy's worries this day. He stayed busy chasing after Jo Bear to keep him from killing all the layers. "Don't you know a fryer from a laying hen?" he screamed after Jo Bear had caught and wrung the neck of a plump Rhode Island matron. "Now, hold off. You see those white Leghorns with some of the tail feathers missing? Them's fryers. Get them and get the big ones. Don't you be killing any more hens. Miz Banks gonna wring both our necks for this."

Thus chastened, Jo Bear was more selective. But he did get one more hen and a banty rooster. Muddy didn't dare criticize, for the real work was at hand, and he needed Jo Bear's help. He knew the volatile boy might up and walk away. And he had already eaten one of his kolaches. The other was for when they had finished.

The boys sat on the steps to pluck the wet feathers from the pile of scalded chickens. Jo Bear raised all kinds of excuses when Muddy insisted he clean the two hens and the rooster. "So you'll know the difference the next time you help."

"The next time? Man, if'n I never see me another chicken, insides or out, I'll not cry. Whew! It sure do stink around here."

"I know. How you gonna carry all those guts to your traps?"

Muddy asked, for the bucket was overflowing by the time they were through. He surveyed the entrails as he pumped water for washing the chickens.

"Forget about them traps. I done decided you and me are gonna bait me the biggest trotline all the way to Taylor's Bayou. And you owe me." He looked at his friend, a scowl of impatience on his freckled face. "This job's worth more than ten cents and a bucket of guts." Muddy didn't answer. He would have agreed to anything, he was so glad the chickens were almost ready. He washed a large keg from the back porch and placed each chicken in it after making certain it was plucked and cleaned thoroughly.

The boys were in the kitchen eating the last of the kolaches when they heard the arrival of the doctor's buggy and the widow's shriek of dismay. "Oh, dear Lord! My chickens! Muddy!" she called. "Muddy Banks, you come here at once!" Muddy and Jo Bear got to the door in time to see the sudden flurry of skirts as the irate woman, not waiting for assistance from the amazed doctor, jumped from the buggy.

Muddy wiped the last crumb of kolache from his face. Grinning broadly, he stepped down from the porch followed closely by Jo Bear. "H'lo, Miz Banks. How's the baby and Miz LeBlanc?"

"Oh Muddy," she wailed. "They're fine, but what have you and Jo Bear done to my fine chickens? Did your alligator get to them? And all those entrails—"

"Calm down, Bethel." Doctor Murray had alighted from the buggy and now stood at her side, with his hand on her shoulder.

"There's bound to be a reasonable explanation for all this." He waved his hand in the direction of the feather-strewn yard. "Although I do admit, I never heard of gutting chickens before feeding them to alligators." Before anything else could be said, Lieutenant Dowling drove up with his team and wagon. He hopped down and tipped his hat to the distraught woman.

"Well, lad, did you fill my order?" He turned to Muddy who in turn pointed to the keg of fryers. Then the boy disappeared into the house for the voucher the lieutenant would sign. While he was gone, the soldier turned to the puzzled adults and explained. "I know I about asked the impossible of your boy, Miz Banks, but I had to have the twenty fryers—"

"Twenty fryers!" gasped the woman.

"Yes, Ma'am. Twenty. General Magruder and his staff are eating with us tonight. We stand inspection at the fort in one hour. So I must hurry back with these." He nodded toward the keg.

"Twenty fryers?" she repeated. "How could he do all I left him to do and dress twenty fryers? Why, it's a miracle!"

"No, Ma'am, Miz Banks. It's me. He hired me to help," beamed Jo Bear, glad to be a part of a suggested miracle. "I helped with the rolls, too." Seeing the look of horror on each face as it gazed at him, he quickly added, "That Muddy made me wash good, with soap, clear up to here." They could see where his clean arms stopped, and began to laugh. "And it was before we cleaned the chickens, too."

"Oh, thank God for that," she murmured.

"Begging your pardon, sir," asked Muddy in a low tone as he handed the voucher to Lieutenant Dowling for his signature, "do you think you would like two fat hens and a banty rooster, too? Makes mighty good dumplings, those hens."

Bethel raised her eyes to her flock of layers out in the chicken yard. "Not my Rhode Island Reds? Oh, Muddy, no."

"It was my fault, Miz Banks." Jo Bear hung his head, admitting guilt. "I never knowed the difference." Both men laughed, not so much at his statement but at the sight of a crestfallen Jo Bear. The whole town was aware of his cockiness and know-it-all ways.

"It's all right, Jo Bear," said the doctor. "I'll buy the hens. Chicken and dumplings sound mighty tasty to me."

"You may buy one," said Bethel. "We'll eat the other one. And Jo Bear, as part of your wages, you can have the banty rooster. At least it'll make good gumbo." She patted Jo Bear on the head as she smiled her approval at Muddy.

Muddy came back from helping haul the chicken entrails down to the *Petit Ami*. This was not much of a chore, since Lieutenant Dowling had let them ride on his wagon on the way back to town. Muddy and Bethel were soon sitting on the back steps talking as they enjoyed the cool afternoon breeze from the Gulf.

When Muddy finished telling her about his day, she asked, "You said Jo Bear helped you for the entrails, ten cents, two kolaches, and his lunch?"

"Yes, Ma'am. And getting to fix the rolls. I think he liked that part best."

"I think it's about time you really started thinking about a real name for yourself. Here you've been a baker, a poultryman, and an employer. No one with those skills need go by the name of Muddy Boy Banks."

"Yes, Ma'am," replied Muddy with a pleased look on his face. "I'm thinking on—about it."

Chapter 13

"YOU COMING, MUDDY?" Jo Bear was standing at the entrance to the barn, watching Muddy curry the mare. The French boy nibbled on a croissant. "How come you take so long?" He swung at a bothersome fly with his free hand. He was in his usual tattered clothing, and except for his clean hands, was as dirt-stained as usual. Bethel had insisted he wash his hands before she gave him the croissant.

Muddy's voice was muffled as he leaned into the flank of the mare, brushing her legs and hooves. "Takes time to do a good job."

"Me, I'd give that old mare a lick and promise and be through. She'll just go out and make a roll around the pasture, I betcha. We've got to git. They'll start and be finished before we get there."

Muddy straightened from his position and sighed. Why did he have to be the one who always had chores to finish before they could play? *If I was free like Jo Bear, I'd never do another chore. No, sir. I'd get me a pirogue, and fish, and sleep, and trap all day.* He untied the mare and turned her toward the pasture. "All right, Jo Bear. I'm ready, now."

"Miz Banks say for you to make a pass by the kitchen and get your croissant before we leave, you hear?" Muddy nodded. The two boys walked to the porch where she stood waiting. Muddy watched as she silently checked to see if he had washed his hands. *Hadn't she seen him at the pump on the way in from the barn? He wasn't no Jo Bear. Even slaves knew to wash their hands.* He sighed. He shouldn't be angry with her. She was doing her best. It was only that he had been fighting himself all morning. First he wanted to go to the fort with Jo Bear. Then he would think about why the fort was there, and he would get angry. Yet when he visited with Lieutenant Dowling, he couldn't stay angry at him, either. Why couldn't they all be on the same side?

He bit into the croissant and smiled his thanks when Bethel offered them a glass of cool milk. The boys sat on the steps while she sat in her rocker, fanning with a palmetto fan.

"Where're you boys headed this afternoon?"

"Up to Fort Griffin, Miz Banks. Jo Bear says the soldiers are going to target practice some."

"Target practice? What targets are they using? There's nothing between their mounts and the horizon except water and the Louisiana marshes."

"There is now," Jo Bear laughed as he said the word.

"Why are you laughing? And don't you story to Miz Banks."

"No, Miz Banks. I ain't funning you none. I was just remembering seeing old Muddy bottom up off'n the end of the pirogue when he was trying to get back into it out by the poles."

"What in the world are you talking about?"

"It was the time we went to the lighthouse, Miz Banks. Didn't Muddy tell you?" He turned to his friend, a devilish glint twinkling in his blue eyes. "Didn't you tell her everything?"

"You hush, Jo Bear. Miz Banks'll think we were in big trouble. And we weren't. I could've swum to shore. I done it before."

"*Did*, Muddy."

"Yes, Ma'am. Did." He hoped she would change the subject.

"Were you in the river and trying to get back into the boat?" Her voice did not sound angry, but she meant business.

He told her what happened the day they had lost their boat at the lighthouse. Jo Bear, for once, was quiet and listened. But he seemed disappointed when she did not get angry.

"How come you don't yell at him like you did when his alligator done ate your setting eggs?"

"I lost my temper that day and I'm sorry. Two dozen setting eggs is a big loss in terms of time and money. But I think Muddy learned a valuable lesson that day about taking care of his pets and having the kind of pets that are suitable. I trust he also learned a lesson when he was out with you in the boat."

"Yes, Ma'am. I did." Muddy was relieved she was not angry. "I learned never to trust this big-mouthed Cajun to do anything right." She appeared shocked at his reference to Jo Bear. But Jo Bear began laughing again. He apparently enjoyed seeing Muddy discomfitted.

"All right, boys, that's enough." Muddy had reached over and shoved Jo Bear off into the grass by the steps, and Jo Bear was trying to wrestle him. "Be still, you two. I want to hear about the targets."

"Yes, Ma'am. I know all about them. That Muddy, he don't know nothing lessen me or you tell him." Bethel placed her hand on the indignant black boy's shoulder, holding him back. He turned and caught the wink she gave him and settled down. *She knows I'm not dumb. Didn't I learn to read and write and work sums?* Muddy consoled himself as he listened to Jo Bear.

Jo Bear grinned slyly as he saw her restraining hand. But he too seemed to know she would not put up with any more foolishness. "See, I'll show you what I meant by the targets." He hopped down and grabbed the chopping axe from the woodpile. Using its keen cutting edge, the Cajun boy drew a rough map in the dirt at the bottom of the steps. Muddy's chest swelled with pride. *Would she recognize the crude map as a copy of the one he had drawn during their studies?* It was the same one they had used on their trip to the lighthouse. He caught her wink and relaxed against the post of the porch. *Let old Jo Bear show off.* He didn't care. He continued to watch as Jo Bear finished the map. Then using a small strip of kindling as a pointer, Jo Bear began to explain.

"See, this here's the fort. See how it sticks out into Sabine Lake and faces on the north end of the channel where it joins the lake? Now, then," he sat back on his heels and looked up at his two students on the porch, "the lieutenant figures the only way his guns can do any damage is to wait until them Yankee ships done come up to here." He marked an *X* on that spot on the map. "And there." He marked another spot with an *X*. "The gunners done told me them cannon don't shoot so good or so far. If'n them Magruder pills gonna hit something, they gotta hit here and here." Again he pointed at the *X*s on the dirt map.

"Magruder pills? What are you talking about, you crazy Cajun?" interrupted Muddy.

"Don't you know anything? That's what the soldiers call the shot they use in their guns. You know, General Magruder—"

"All I remember about that general is how we had to fix all those fryers for them when Miz Banks was gone up to Taylor's Bayou." Bethel joined in the laughter and then explained about General Magruder's being in charge of the Confederate forces in their part of Texas. She told them how the artillerymen had nicknamed their shot during the battle for Galveston when General Magruder had been in command. It was in this battle, earlier that year, that General Magruder and his men had recaptured Galveston from the Union forces. "Yes, boys, in these parts, Magruder pills are well-known."

"But I still don't remember seeing targets—oh, now I remember," said Muddy. "Those were the marking poles set in the water, weren't they? That's what they have to shoot toward. Right?"

"Right. See, Miz Banks, the Davis Guards done stuck them poles down where they expect to hit a ship if it comes sailing into Sabine Lake. 'Scuse us, Miz Banks. Come on, Muddy. We gotta go. Thanks for the croissants."

"Thanks," said Muddy, too. But he pronounced the "th" with great emphasis, hoping Miz Banks would realize he was trying to say his words correctly. She smiled as though she understood and waved the boys off to their next adventure.

"Stay out of the way," she called to them.

They set off at a brisk dogtrot down the shell road. Muddy's feet were as tough as Jo Bear's, and the shell no longer bothered him. It didn't take them long to cover the half-mile to the fort. Muddy was eager to see the fort up close. Until now his resentment toward the soldiers who were there to fight to keep him a slave had kept him away. But his curiosity won out and at last he was to see the fort in action, even if it were only practice firing.

Nearing the fort, they could hear the men shouting directions to each other as they readied the artillery for firing. As the boys reached the near side of the earthenworks, Jo Bear clamped his hands over his ears. Muddy did, too, not taking time to ask why. He was glad he did, for one of the crews had loaded its cannon, and the sudden order of "Fire!" came. The huge gun on the rampart belched smoke and fire and the loudest noise Muddy had ever heard. Even with his ears covered, his head rang from the noise of the explosion. Jo Bear, no stranger to these artillery practices, was pointing excitedly toward the river. The splash was over close to the Louisiana shore.

"He's way off. Lieutenant Dowling is going to be some mad, him." The crew lowered the nose of the gun and primed it to fire again. "This time I betcha they don't miss, Muddy." Muddy was too busy watching to wager. The men were well trained and worked as a team. Soon the order to "Fire!" rang out again. Muddy braced himself for the explosion again. The noise didn't seem to bother him as much this second time. As Jo Bear had predicted, the shot landed near enough to the pole to knock it down.

"Bull's-eye!" yelled the men. They seemed to be keeping score on each gun. Each time they fired, their accuracy improved. Soon no pole remained. Lieutenant Dowling called a halt to the firing. He ordered the company to clean up and ready the cannon for inspection. As the lieutenant inspected each mount—there were only six—Jo Bear told Muddy what kind it was.

"He's got two twenty-four pounder smooth bores. Then there are the thirty-two pounder howitzers—"

"What is that? Howi—?"

"It's a kind of cannon. We'll get one of the men to explain when they finish inspection."

"Are we going right up where the men are?"

"Sure, Muddy. They like to talk about their cannon. I saw Mr. Smith pat his just like you pat your mare. Now let me finish about the cannon. There's two thirty-two pounder smooth bores. Lieutenant Dowling done told me those mavourneens can shoot a mile and half." Jo Bear, who took the job of teacher very seriously, was pointing at each gun as he named it.

"Mavourneen? That their name?"

"No, that's Irish talk. I don't know what it means. I wish they talked good like me." He turned, a puzzled look on his face, at the sound of Muddy's laughter at his last remark. When he gave Muddy a shove, nearly toppling him from his perch, Muddy did not retaliate. Miz Banks had cautioned him not to hurt Jo Bear's feelings about the way he spoke English.

He asked instead, "How far are the poles from here?"

"' Bout one thousand yards, the gunner say."

"How wide is this part of the channel?"

"'Bout three thousand yards, I think. Come over here out of the way." Jo Bear pulled Muddy along with him until they were standing on the northernmost side.

"This solid dirt?" Muddy stomped his foot, as though to test the strength of the embankment.

"Dirt? No, not solid dirt. They took the timbers off'n that Yankee ship, *The Morning Light*. You know, the ship the Yanks abandoned when we fought them back in January. They're in this dirt.

And they took up some of the track by Miz Banks' house and put two layers of them in this dirt. Me, I watched them build it all. See those five holes? They got two feet of timber inside of them, too. That foreign colonel sure did crack them orders, and the men really worked."

"It's really not a very big fort, is it?" Muddy was disappointed. He had expected a tour of a more elaborate defense.

"Big enough. I 'spect those Irishmen can fight good enough without much. They know how to aim those guns, believe you me."

One of the soldiers, seeing the boys, came up to talk. Jo Bear approached him. "Say, Mister, could you tell my friend, Muddy Banks here, about your cannon? He don't know nothing like me." Muddy, embarrassed, wanted to turn and go. But he also wanted to hear what the soldier had to say, so he swallowed his pride.

"Sure, and I'll tell you about our pets, here." He took the boys around to each cannon and began to explain its use and type. Muddy was hard put to understand what the man was saying. His accent was heavy and foreign to Muddy's ear. Still, he did not interrupt. He wanted to learn all that he could. Lieutenant Dowling spotted them and came over and rubbed their heads.

"The two poultrymen," he said as he greeted them. The men laughed, for they had been told how the boys got the fryers ready for General Magruder's dinner. Muddy wasn't offended by their laughter because he realized they meant no harm. In fact, he was afraid he was beginning to like these strange men who were his enemies. He would have to ask Miz Banks about that. How could you like your enemies?

Soon the soldiers were through polishing and cleaning their cannon. The ammunition was properly stored. The boys hated to leave as they watched the boisterous soldiers assemble in straggly formation and march toward their quarters. Muddy heaved a sigh of regret and turned toward the house. Maybe there wouldn't be a battle, after all. He wanted to be free, but he didn't want a battle.

Chapter 14

SEVERAL MORNINGS later, Muddy woke with a start. Horses! The sound of hard-running horses had jarred him awake. At least two, he guessed. He leaned out his window, but they were already out of sight around the bend. *Why the hurry? Oh, well, I'll find out in the morning.* He snuggled back into his pillow and dropped back into an easy sleep.

But it didn't last long. He woke again to an insistent whistling outside his window. It had to be Jo Bear. What was happening? First the horses tearing down the road toward Beaumont, and now Jo Bear out of bed before sunup. And it wasn't even the day the *Petit Ami* was due to go out. He leaned out the window and whispered, "What do you want?"

"Git up! Them Yanks are up to no good. Come on down." Muddy stared at Jo Bear through the murkiness of the dawn. Jo Bear was so excited he was practically dancing a jig.

"Don't talk so loud. You'll wake Miz Banks."

"Wake Miz Banks? Why, Muddy, the whole town's awake 'cepting you. Now come on down. Miz Banks' kitchen lamp is burning. I'll meet you there." Stunned, Muddy watched the exultant boy disappear around the side of the house. Then he looked at his watch. Four-thirty! The early hour galvanized him into action. In minutes he was washed, dressed, and in the kitchen. The widow was questioning the excited Jo Bear.

"Jo Bear, you'll have to speak slower. I can't understand."

"It's the Yanks! They're here!"

"In Sabine City?"

"No'm, not yet, that is. But they're coming. The couriers woke Captain Pete and told him to get ready. The Yanks are signaling back 'n forth out in the Gulf."

Bethel slumped against the cabinet. "I ought to wring your neck, Jo Bear Prejean. From the way you were acting, I thought they were outside my back door." She shook her finger in his face, but Muddy could tell she was not angry, only scared.

Before Jo Bear could answer, a voice from the back door spoke. It was Doctor Murray. "Don't shoot, Bethel. It's only me." Doctor Murray came in, pulled up a chair to the table, and sat down.

Things are happening too fast around here to suit me, decided Muddy. He leaned against the wall, waiting to hear what would happen next. His shoulder rattled the calendar hanging behind him, and he turned to mark the day. Using the pencil tied to a string hanging from the same nail that held the calender, he saw that this new day, September 7, 1863, was no holiday. Carefully he crossed out the previous day, as he had learned to do this when Miz Banks taught him about days and weeks and months.

"Muddy, do you hear me?" Miz Banks was talking to him.

"No'm, yes'm. I was just marking the day." He walked over to where Jo Bear was seated at the table and pulled up a chair.

"I want you all to hush talking at the same time. We're going to listen to what Doctor Murray has to say. And, Jo Bear, don't interrupt him. You can tell what you know when he's done." She poured coffee for them and a cupful for herself before sitting down to face the others across the table. "All right, now, Doctor Murray. What's all this talk about the Yankees being right here and furthermore, why are you here?" That was what Muddy had been wondering all along. The doctor must have a purpose for being there at that time of morning.

"The Yanks aren't here, Bethel. But," he put out a restraining hand on the objecting Jo Bear, "there's a mighty good chance they will be before long. The couriers along the coast spotted their signal lights several hours ago. They have gone to give the word to General Magruder and his staffs at Beaumont and Orange." *The horsemen,* thought Muddy, *they were on their way when they woke me up.*

But the doctor continued. "Whether or not we are invaded depends on the performance of Colonel Joseph J. Cook's Company F of the First Heavy Artillery Regiment." He rose to his feet and lifted his cup of coffee in a salute to the gallant men.

"Company F? I thought the Irishmen were going to fight the Yankees." Muddy was upset. Were there going to be more soldiers to keep him from being free?

"That's their official designation, Muddy. But it's going to take more than a fancy name like that to keep all those warships out of Sabine Lake."

Jo Bear had kept quiet until the doctor had said that. "They can do it. The Davis Guards can do it. Me, I just know they can." He was pounding the table with his spoon.

"Now, Jo Bear, calm down. Muddy, don't look so glum. It isn't the end of the world," Bethel said. "I'm going to fix everyone some breakfast."

Muddy grinned at her. He remembered her saying, "An idle mind's the devil's workshop." Perhaps the devil was coming up the river.

"Let me finish," said Doctor Murray. "So far, none of the ships has crossed the bar. But it may be a matter of waiting on the proper tide. Now I'll tell you why I'm here. And, thank you, Bethel, I'd enjoy a good breakfast." As she turned to the stove and began frying the ham, the doctor leaned back in his chair and looked at the boys. "We knew the Yankees would try to invade Texas. In fact, nearly all the Texas men have been sent to the Red River to mass there at the Arkansas Station. That's where our military seem to think the Union troops will try to penetrate. Whole towns in East Texas have sent every available man to that front. But Captain Odlum told me this morning our side must have figured wrong. For all those lights out there can mean only one thing." He paused, drank his coffee, then continued. "It's a regular armada."

"Armada? What kind of ship a armada be, Doctor Murray?" Jo Bear's eyes were large and questioning.

"It's not a ship. It's a word used to describe a large fleet of warships about to engage in battle. Captain Odlum says this has to be the invasion the Texans have been expecting. The troops will be landing here instead of coming across from Louisiana at the Red River."

Muddy was overjoyed. Here was the answer to his dilemma. The time was at hand for him to run away. Now he wouldn't have to leave Jo Bear and Miz Banks. He would be free, but he would still be in Sabine City. Joy at that thought was short-lived when he saw the look on Miz Banks' face.

"Then that means we aren't prepared." Bethel stood over them with her egg turner held high. Muddy could tell she was really worried. A surge of fear swept through him. *Miz Banks was scared of Yankees? Did she think the soldiers who would come ashore might hurt her? Would they?* He knew she could not run and hide; she must be fifty years old.

Distress tinged his voice as he turned toward the doctor. "Would they hurt women?" He ducked his head, embarrassed by this display of emotion. Bethel paused and looked at him, then turned quickly back to the stove and her cooking.

"I don't think they would purposely hurt women, especially Bethel. She'll be with me helping with the wounded." The doctor's voice was calm as he spoke. "Of course, if there is a battle, any of us could get hurt by a stray bullet, an exploding shell, or fires that come from lamps being hit. Bethel was lucky last time. Though her water tank and barn were hit, there were no fires. And," he shook his head with disgust, "there are times when troops ransack and pillage and set fire to every building in sight. We must take precautions and plan our activities."

"You're going to eat, first." Bethel set plates of ham, eggs, and grits in front of the boys and Doctor Murray. "Muddy, you get the pitcher of milk from the cooler." Then she sat down. After Muddy returned with the milk, the doctor offered thanks for the meal even as he entreated the Almighty to watch over and protect each one present. Muddy liked the idea of being under the watch of the Lord.

They ate silently, each one deep in thought about the approaching day. Jo Bear finished first. "I'm going down to the fort," he announced, pushing his chair back from the table.

The doctor's stern command to "Sit down!" stopped him. He meekly resumed his seat at the table and waited. So did Muddy, who had finished eating, too. After one more gulp of coffee, the doctor stood up.

"That's one of the main reasons I'm here, Jo Bear. I intend to see you stay away from that fort. You, too, Muddy Banks. No," he said, anticipating Jo Bear's protest. "I mean exactly what I say. I want you to get on that shrimp boat with Captain Placette and go with him. He's going to Orange for reinforcements. He's going to put you and Muddy—yes, Muddy, you are going too—off at the LeBlancs' at Taylor's Bayou. I know they will have room for you and will hide you both, if necessary." Muddy and Jo Bear would not be silenced. Both pleaded with the doctor and Bethel, alternately.

"I want to stay with Miz Banks, Doctor Murray. I can tote water. I can." Then a thought occurred to him. *Why do I have to hide? They're coming to free me.* The doctor looked at Bethel and shook his head.

"And me, I can help put out fires and carry water to keep the guns cool. I'm almost full-growed," insisted Jo Bear. "And I can fire my pappa's musket."

"Ha! That old thing?" Muddy and Jo Bear fell to arguing about the merits of the old firepiece that, along with the pirogue, was Jo Bear's entire inheritance.

Finally Doctor Murray roared for silence. "You both are being foolish. But it seems you want to stay. Then stay."

"Hurrah!" yelled the boys before the doctor could continue his instructions for them.

"Quiet! And listen. And sit down. If you stay, you will do exactly what I tell you. And don't interrupt me. I'm behind schedule. I have other places to visit, you know."

Muddy thought the doctor sounded angry. *Maybe he's only blustering. He likes us, I know. I'd best be quiet, though.* He kicked out at Jo Bear when he started to speak. Jo Bear threw him an indignant look, but subsided into his chair as they waited for the doctor's instructions.

"Now, boys, I want you to pump the tank full of water. I want you to fill every vessel you can find and place them around the house. I want water handy in case of fire. Then you can go about your chores." He must have seen the sly smile on Jo Bear's face, for he added, "and Jo Bear, you'll help Muddy get his chores done. You two will stay together at all times. Do you understand? Jo Bear? Muddy?"

Both boys nodded. *What else can a boy do when the grown-ups lay the law down—especially a slave boy.* Muddy chased the bitter thought away. *Bet I won't be a slave for long,* he gloated silently. The doctor had called his rescuers an armada and that had to mean a bunch.

"As soon as the chores are done, and if the fighting hasn't started," Doctor Murray was shaking his finger in Jo Bear's face, "then, and only then," now his finger was in front of Muddy's face, "can you go down to the fort to see if you can help. Don't—" But his last words were drowned in the shouts of the boys. They were jumping up and down. The doctor pulled Bethel out to the porch and began talking. The boys noticed and hushed. Muddy wanted to hear, and so did Jo Bear.

". . . and bring all your salves and ointment. Bring pure lard that has not been used. Do you have any bandage-making materials? I don't know if Doctor Bailey will be bringing in additional medical supplies from Galveston."

"Yes, I have some sheets," they heard her reply. "If you don't send for me sooner, I'll finish my noon baking and come down with my supplies."

"That will be fine. Now I must go. Jo Bear! Where are you going? Come back here this instant!" The wily boy had slipped through the back door and was sneaking off the porch behind the doctor's back. Muddy knew Jo Bear had not planned on helping him with the chores. He tried to keep a straight face as he watched the doctor grab Jo Bear by the collar. "And just where do you think you're going, young man?" He gave the boy's shoulder a good shaking.

"Ah, me, Doctor Murray. I was going to run down to the fort

for one small minute just to see. Then I was coming right back to help my good friend, Muddy, to do them chores." Jo Bear rolled his big, blue, innocent eyes up at the doctor. "It'll be a long time before the firing starts, I betcha," he pleaded.

"I don't know when the firing will begin. I don't rightly know when the tide will permit those ships to come through the Pass." He paused to give Jo Bear another shake. "Now, listen to me. There are two big steamers standing off the Pass. They are obviously sounding it and will sound the channel, too. There is only six feet of water there at best. I don't know the draft of the warships. In fact, I don't know anything except that you two are going to do exactly what I told you to do. Right?" Both boys nodded their heads vigorously. Doctor Murray did not seem certain of their promises to obey his orders, for he turned loose of Jo Bear's collar and shook his finger in Jo Bear's face. "And if you don't do what I said, I'll put you back in that Calcasieu orphanage. You can bet those good sisters won't let you set foot on a boat until you are sixteen years old." Jo Bear's face paled at the doctor's threat.

He's convinced, thought Muddy. And he was glad. He wanted to be with Jo Bear if there was a battle.

Muddy set Jo Bear to feeding and watering the stock while he did the milking. He knew it would take too long to show Jo Bear how Miz Banks handled the fresh milk. There were so many things to learn to do when working around her. And most of them were woman's work. *When I'm free, I'm gonna work for a man. I'm gonna learn to do only man's work. Maybe I'll work on the railroad, or on a ship and go to China with Jo Bear. When I'm free—* Muddy laid his head against the flank of the friendly Jersey cow, his milking forgotten as he dreamed of freedom.

"Muddy!" called Jo Bear. "Come on!" Muddy gave a couple more tugs at the now deflated udder. *Daydreams will have to wait. This is living time. Maybe, by tomorrow, I'll be free and then—*he stood up, shaking his head. His young mind could not handle that tremendous prospect.

"Wait until I pour up and wash the buckets, Jo Bear," he called, relieved to be absorbed in the ordinary tasks at hand.

Chapter 15

THE BOYS pumped water until their arms ached. Every pot and vessel was filled and placed about the house, inside and out. When they had finished their chores, Bethel was well into her noon roll-baking. She was also baking pies and cakes. Every surface in the large kitchen was covered with pastry, rolls, or cake fixings. Muddy gave a silent prayer of thanks for the brisk breeze. The windmill was now turning and filling the large storage tank. At least he and Jo Bear wouldn't have to do that. They gathered and washed the eggs. Muddy's bed was made. This finished their chores. They ran down into the kitchen to take turns reciting their deeds to Bethel.

"You two may go down to the fort. But—" she started to add, and it was too late. The boys had jumped from the back of the porch and were racing toward the fort. She shook her head knowingly and smiled as she returned to her kitchen.

Jo Bear and Muddy ran all the way. They were out of breath when they threw themselves on the northern incline of the four-foot-high redoubt. Their heads were barely visible over the top as they looked down on the Guards and the townspeople milling around.

"Looks like a speaking," gasped Jo Bear. "Never saw so many people 'cept around 'lection time."

"Yeah. Some of them is in the way, too."

"Bet the lieutenant don't allow that for long." Jo Bear was regaining some of his cockiness.

Then a man yelled, "There's some Yankee ships in the channel, now!" The crowd of citizens surged toward the banks of the river to watch the ships' progress up the channel. Lieutenant Dowling tried to disperse the crowd. He urged them to seek shelter back in town. Muddy and Jo Bear ducked their heads from view.

"We can stay here as long as they don't see us," cautioned Jo Bear. The Guards were manning their guns, ready to fire on the invaders. When the boys heard the men begin to grumble, Jo Bear sneaked a peek.

"Why, those old Yankee ships are pure-D yellow," he complained. Muddy looked, not believing. But they were. All nine steamers that had crossed into the channel were coming about and heading back out to sea. *It's really a picnic, not a war,* he decided, disgusted with the forces he had hoped had come to free him. Now the ladies of the town were bringing food and coffee to the Guards. The Guards were laughing and teasing each other about their great battle.

Finally Muddy said, "I'm going home. Ain't gonna be no fight. Just play-like stuff." He emptied his pockets of the shells he had gathered to chunk at the water. They had been entertaining themselves by seeing who could throw the farthest. "You coming?"

"No. I gonna stay and listen to the men. The ships might come back."

"Sure they will. And it might come a blizzard, too." He was heartsick and embarrassed by the performance of his rescuers. Walking slowly, with his head hanging down, he ignored the merrymakers along the road back to town. He didn't go into the house but slipped into the section house and crawled through the opening to the attic where he untied the corners of the blanket to stare at his "needs." The boots, the clothing, the tins of food, and his map were just as he had left them.

One more day. I'll give you Yanks one more day to free me. I can't wait any longer. Winter's coming. He slowly retied the blanket that held his cache. Would his mammy have understood about his not wanting to leave Miz Banks? Before going to the kitchen, he pulled out the cage with his pet alligator from under the house. "Something's gonna get freed today," he mumbled, "even if it isn't me."

He ran down to the shore and released the alligator. The alligator must have sensed its free meals would cease. It tried to follow the dejected boy. Twice Muddy had to return it to the mudflat. The pet, finally tired, began to bury itself in the mud. *Dumb old 'gator. Don't even want to be free.*

Bethel did not question him when he returned. She, too, had seen the ships turn back. "It's over, I guess," she said in a way of greeting. "Thank goodness no one was injured."

"Ain't no one freed, either," he mumbled as he pulled a book from the shelf and went upstairs to study.

That evening they were sitting on the seldom-used front porch. It was an effort for each to swat mosquitoes and stay cool at the same time. Muddy straddled the porch railing staring in the direction of the fort. Every now and then he would stand on the railing for a better view. Yet all he could see were the lamps bobbing about at the fort in the hands of the people walking back toward town.

"Seems to me the scare is over, Muddy."

"Yes, Ma'am. Guess so." They began to hear faint whistling heralding the approach of Jo Bear. Muddy had not seen him since leaving the fort. "Hi! That you, Jo Bear?"

The whistling stopped, then started again. Jo Bear was trying to whistle "Dixie." They laughed at his efforts. The tune was hardly recognizable.

"He must be whistling it in French," teased Bethel. Before Muddy could ask her what she meant, Jo Bear appeared in the road in front of the house. "Come on the porch," called Bethel. He came and sat on the steps, bracing his back against one of the pillars. "Tell us," she asked, "is there any news of the ships? Muddy and I haven't left the house all evening."

"No'm, there ain't. From what I could gather—"

"Snoop," interrupted Muddy.

"I don't neither snoop. Everyone was shouting back and forth. Weren't no need to snoop."

"All right, boys. Muddy, that wasn't nice. I asked for information."

"Miz Banks, he'll probably make it all up."

"Muddy, I don't know why you're in such a bad humor. I want Jo Bear to tell me what he heard. If you don't care to listen, I suggest you go on up to bed. I never saw you like this before."

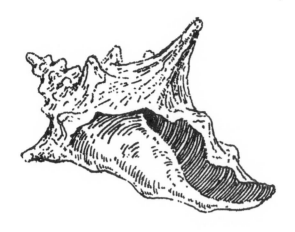

"Oh, he's sore 'cause them Yankees are cowards and won't come and fight." Muddy came off the railing and immediately both boys were rolling in the grass with fists swinging.

"That's enough of that!" The boys jumped to their feet, for they recognized her you've-gone-too-far voice. "Sit down, both of you. Muddy, am I—"

"No, Ma'am. I'll behave."

"All right. Jo Bear, what were you saying?"

"Well, them couriers Captain Odlum done sent out to the telegraph stations to warn everyone, they come back. The Irishmen are real sore. General Magruder told the captain to blow up the fort. He don't want no one killed here. He say, fall back to Taylor's Bayou."

"What did Captain Odlum say to that?"

"I guess he say 'No!' for the Davis Guards are spending the night up there at the fort. Ain't nobody falling back."

"Retreating, you mean."

"Yes'm. I guess so. Doctor Bailey is gonna stay there, and Lieutenant Smith, that new engineer, he's gonna be there, too. The men are playing cards and drinking coffee."

"So General Magruder wants them to abandon the fort and go

to Taylor's Bayou. Just like they did when the old fort was attacked last October."

Muddy didn't say anything. *Let the white folks figure out their problems.* He had his own.

"General Magruder's smart," bragged Jo Bear. "But Captain Odlum, he ain't no quitter. Not like some—"

Muddy did not let Jo Bear finish his insult. "They'd better listen to him. They'll all get killed if they stay at the fort." Muddy was hoping for a sign of weakness on the part of the South.

"Whooee, black boy. You better not let any of those soldiers hear that. They're so eager to start shooting, I 'spect they're praying those silly Yankees show themselves right now."

Bethel stood and placed her hand on Muddy's shoulder. "Well, we won't argue about it. It's past time for you boys to be in bed. Muddy, go upstairs and get some of Jed's clothes for Jo Bear and

clean clothes for you, too. Jo Bear, you collect the soap and towels from the back porch. This may be the last chance you boys have to take a good bath for awhile. We don't know when we may be driven from our home." The boys began mumbling about the enforced bathing. "Now, hurry! Not a word from either of you. I want both of you in the tank within three minutes. If you're not, I'll personally supervise your baths." She did not have to threaten further. They took off running.

While they were stripping down by the tank, Jo Bear whined, "I don't need me a bath. I took me a swim this morning."

"With soap?" heckled Muddy. But he left the white boy alone and didn't try to duck him. Jo Bear, cowed by Bethel's threat to supervise, started scrubbing furiously. Muddy kept thinking about the other thing she had said. "Driven from our home." That frightened him. He had not considered that possibility. All he had thought about was having the Yanks appear to set him free. He had figured things would be the same in Sabine City when that happened. But she talked as though things would be terrible. This was her home. He wanted her to be all right, not driven out somewhere.

The boys dressed and walked back toward the house. Jo Bear was still fussing about the bath. Muddy couldn't help but laugh. That Jo Bear was something else. Didn't he know being free didn't mean you should give up taking baths? He began to tease Jo Bear once they were inside the house. Bethel quickly intervened. The boys were sent to bed.

"I want no more fighting, you hear?" she admonished. "I have to get up early. If you don't go to bed and be quiet, I promise you I'll get you both up when I get up, and you'll begin your chores at once." This was threat enough. The boys took her at her word and were soon fast asleep.

Chapter 16

MUDDY woke to the sound of dishes clattering in the kitchen. He turned his sleepy eyes toward the window. It was still dark outside. Were the Yanks coming back? He jumped from the bed and ran into the bedroom across the hall. "Jo Bear! Wake up! There's people in the kitchen." He shook him firmly but gently as he whispered. He did not want his buddy to wake up screaming. Those voices in the kitchen might be Yanks.

Jo Bear opened one eye and peered at Muddy. "Why for you wake me up?"

He doesn't remember about the Yanks, I'll bet. "There's people in the kitchen. Maybe the Yanks are here."

Jo Bear bounded from the bed, grabbing for his clothes. "They're here?"

"Someone's here." Muddy returned to his own room and dressed. Then the boys slipped down the stairs and peeked into the kitchen. The visitors were only Doctor Murray and Moses.

Oh, no, is this going to be another day for pumping water and doing chores? Jo Bear must have had the same thought, for he groaned aloud.

"Come on in, boys. I was just about to waken you." Bethel smiled as though it were any other day. Muddy walked over to the calendar and crossed out September 7. It had been a wasted day for getting his freedom. He wondered what September 8, 1863 would bring. The Yankees, he hoped. He and Jo Bear went out back and soon reappeared, washed and ready for the new day. Moses had finished loading his cart.

Muddy walked to the back porch with him and whispered to the old man, "Maybe the Yankees come back and free us today."

"You kinda crazy, boy. Old Moses don't want to be free. Who'd feed old Moses if'n he don't belong to nobody? Yankees don't want old Moses. I belong to the hotel. Miz Kate allus take good care of old Moses like her pappy did before her."

"But you're a slave, Moses. You mean you like being owned by somebody?" Muddy was aghast. He thought all negroes felt as he did.

"Ah like it just like it is. Now, boy, get out'n my way. These rolls gotta git to the hotel. Miz Kate done skin me alive if'n I bring them cold."

"If you're free, no white woman gonna skin you alive."

"Hush yo' mouth, Muddy Boy Banks. You talk foolishment." Moses pushed the cart toward the hotel, shaking his kinky-gray head.

Muddy felt like crying. He thought Moses would be happy to be free. His face was glum as he entered the kitchen. He sat down at the table and stared at the food placed before him.

"Why so sad, Muddy?" asked Doctor Murray.

"It's nothing, sir."

Jo Bear wolfed his eggs and bacon but paused long enough to say, "Old Muddy, he's 'shamed about the Yankees being cowards."

"Don't talk with your mouth full, Jo Bear." Bethel's voice was sharp.

Muddy looked at her. It wasn't like her to speak so to anyone, especially company. But then he saw the look of compassion on her face, and he knew it was for him. *She's afraid Jo Bear's hurt my feelings.* He understood why she had spoken so. He straightened in his chair. He had to ask.

"Miz Banks, how come Miz Kate's Moses don't want to be free?" Doctor Murray put down his cup and glanced at her. She seemed to study Muddy's question awhile, then turned to the doctor.

"How do I explain that?"

"Let me try." He got up and poured himself another cup of coffee before walking over to the window to stare out toward the channel. He turned in a moment and leaned against the cabinet. Then he began to speak. "Muddy, every man wants to be free.

It's his inherent right under the Constitution. Thank God, slavery in the South is gradually disappearing. Many owners are freeing their slaves." Muddy couldn't help but show his surprise at this information.

"Do you know any? Freed slaves, I mean?"

"No, Muddy. I don't. There aren't too many freed slaves in this part of Texas. In fact, a freed slave here would probably be kidnapped by unscrupulous men and resold." He paused to shake his head in disgust.

Muddy's eyes widened. *How could they do that to freed slaves?* This was something he had never heard of before. *Would someone grab him and resell him?* But Doctor Murray was speaking again. Muddy didn't want to miss a word.

"Most of the older slaves like Moses are well-treated and respected. Moses knows he will be taken care of no matter what befalls him. He's considered family. If he were free, he would have no place to go. His wife is buried in the town cemetery. His children are grown and were sold to out-of-town buyers. All he has is Miz Kate and the hotel. It's his life. If he were younger and realized there might be another kind of life for him, I'm certain he, too, would want to be free."

"Me, I'm free lak a bird! Jo Bear Prejean, me, myself. I belong to nobody." Muddy looked at his excited friend. But Jo Bear seemed serious, not bragging. *Does he finally understand how I've felt about being owned?*

Bethel poured more milk into the white boy's glass as she asked, "But, Jo Bear, what good would your freedom be if Captain Placette did not take care of you?"

The boy looked up at her with a surprised look on his face. "Me, I take care of myself. I can hunt and fish and swim and row—"

"And each night you bed down in your clean berth on the *Petit Ami*," interrupted Doctor Murray. "Each morning there is food on the table cooked by Captain Placette. When you need clothes there are clothes for you."

Muddy smiled at the doctor. Now he understood about Moses.

Then another thought crossed his mind. He turned to Bethel. "If I—"

But she shook her head and smiled. "We'll cross that bridge when we get to it. Now eat your breakfast."

"Yes, and eat plenty. Bethel, perhaps you'd better pack some staples and have them ready. There was much signaling again around two o'clock this morning."

"They're back! Do you hear that, Jo Bear. They're back! The Yankees are back." Muddy pounded his buddy on the back. He could not keep the happiness from his voice. Then he realized he was the only one at the table who was happy. He sat down, and his face grew solemn, too.

Jo Bear, once he recovered from the pommeling Muddy had given him, had half-risen from his chair in his excitement.

"There's no rush, Jo Bear," said Bethel. "Stop stuffing your mouth so full."

"Yes, Muddy, they're back." Doctor Murray's tone was grim, but Muddy wouldn't think about the other side. He waited for the doctor to continue. "The ships are slowly but surely coming up the channel today." The doctor put his cup down and placed his hand on Jo Bear's shoulder. "Whoa there, young man. And where do you think you're going?"

"Please, Doctor Murray, please let me go down to the fort."

"Sorry, son. No civilians allowed. The *Clifton* is already up close enough to commence firing. She has the fort within her range.

"But I want to see her!"

"No. Now, remember what I told you two yesterday. The same holds true for today." He stared at them before turning to the widow. "I suggest you bake as fast and as much as you can before the firing starts. Then you had better extinguish your ovens and come up to my office."

"Yes, Doctor. We'll do as we're told, won't we boys? Whether we want to or not," she added with a chuckle, seeing their woeful expressions.

With Jo Bear helping, it did not take long to do Muddy's

chores. They did not have to pump water. The tank and vessels were still filled from the day before. About six-thirty, just as they were resting on the back porch, the cannon from the *Clifton* roared. The boys and the widow ran out into the road in front of the house for a better view. Bethel clung to Jo Bear who was begging to be allowed to go to the fort. Again the cannon roared.

"Jo Bear," she urged, "climb up on the roof of the porch and see if the fort's been hit." He needed no further prompting. He scampered up one of the supporting pillars and clawed his way up the rough, shingled roof.

"Boom!" went the cannon again.

"They missed! Overshot!"

"Boom!" again.

"Missed again. Too short, this time."

"Please, Miz Banks. Let me go, too," pleaded Muddy. She gave him a shove in the direction of the house. He made it to the roof but not as easily as the nimble Jo Bear. For an hour, the *Clifton* kept shelling the fort but failed to register a hit. The boys begged to be allowed to climb to the widow's walk on top of the house.

"No, you'll fall and break an arm or leg. We have steps from the attic to the roof, but it's still too high for you. Anyway, you might get hit." Muddy was thinking she'd be hard put to keep them off the widow's walk when she left to go to the doctor's office.

However, the *Clifton* stopped firing after an hour. Jo Bear reported it was turning about and heading back down the channel toward the Pass. When Miz Banks heard this, she called the boys down from the porch roof. "Come on inside. You two can help me with my baking. We've wasted enough time as it is."

"Wonder why Lieutenant Dowling didn't return fire," asked Muddy as they descended the porch roof.

"Range not close enough. The lieutenant and the captain know what to do. They're laying low. When the warships get even with them poles, you'll really hear a racket." Jo Bear hurried Muddy into the kitchen. "Let's get through here so we can go back on the roof."

He winked at Muddy. Muddy knew his buddy was thinking about the same thing—the widow's walk.

The boys helped. The kitchen was awhirl with flour, but Bethel did not complain. She finally declared a rest period for the boys when the rolls were in the oven. "It'll take me fifteen minutes to prepare the pie fillings. Why don't you two go out on the back porch and rest?" Muddy joined Jo Bear in pleading for permission to go up on the widow's walk. Finally she consented.

She led them up the stairs to the attic. A circular iron staircase led to the trap door in the roof. Jo Bear, eager to be the first on the rooftop, pushed ahead of Muddy. Jerking on the metal handle, he opened the door, only to be rewarded for his shoving with a shower of dust and cobwebs. He stepped back to wipe the dust from his eyes. Muddy seized the opportunity to get to the rooftop first.

"If you two are going to fight, you can come down right this minute!" Bethel called up to them. Both boys promised there would be no fighting. *We mean it, too. This is too wonderful a thing to mess up by fighting,* decided Muddy. *We can fight anytime, but not now.*

The view from the widow's walk was all they had imagined. They could see everything. "It's better than the lighthouse, Jo Bear." Muddy was struck by the beauty of the day. The sky, a bright blue, made a perfect background for the gliding of the seagulls overhead. A few clouds, shaped like bolls of cotton, tumbled across the sky, pushed by capricious winds. *It certainly did not look like a war sky,* mused Muddy. *Thunder and lightning makes a war sky.*

His buddy seemed oblivious to his feelings. He was busy studying the channel below. "Miz Banks," he called to the waiting figure at the bottom of the steps, "there's seven of them."

"Seven of what?"

"Transports, Miz Banks, transports." Muddy was glad Jo Bear was relaying the information. He did not know what the vessels were. He only knew they were awesome looking. There were seven: the *Suffolk*, the *St. Charles*, the *Landis*, the *Exact*, the *Thomas*, the *Laurel Hill*, and the *General Banks*. The Union transports were anchored out of range, carrying over two thousand troops. Their captains waited patiently for signals to proceed.

"You'd better come down, boys."

They insisted there was no immediate danger until the ships came within range. "Please, Miz Banks, the minute they begin firing, we'll come down, honest," promised Muddy. She agreed to let them stay until she needed them with the baking. Jo Bear was beside himself with anticipation.

"Come on, you Billy Yanks," he shouted over the rooftop. "Come and get a taste of what we're cooking up for you." Muddy did not say anything. He couldn't see how the little fort could withstand such a host of ships, but his side had let him down before. He didn't intend to do any premature gloating. He was taking no chances on having to eat crow served up by Jo Bear.

True to her word, Bethel called them back to the kitchen to help roll the piecrusts. But she let them take turns running up to the roof to see what was taking place down on the channel. There was no firing. An unnatural quiet had settled over the community. Finally around nine-thirty, she told the boys they could run down to the fort.

The hot sun moved toward the zenith as the panting boys arrived at the fort. They mingled with the throng until they found a good spot to rest and catch their breath. Muddy studied his watch. *It's nearly eleven o'clock, and a workday, but the townspeople are still acting like it's a holiday.* He and Jo Bear began circling the perimeter of the fort. No one was permitted inside. Lieutenant Dowling and Captain Odlum stood at the edge of the water, conferring. They walked back to the embankment and climbed to its highest point. Muddy and Jo Bear raced for the nearest wagon and climbed up on the seat.

They saw small boats being lowered from the *Sachem*. Each was loaded with soldiers in full battle garb. The boys watched as the boats approached the site of the old, abandoned fort.

When the boats were about 125 feet from shore, the unsuspecting helmsman bogged the boats in the muddy flats below the surface of the murky waters. The Irish gun crews begged Lieutenant Dowling to let them fire on the boats. But no such order came from Dowling. Jo Bear began laughing with the crowd as it jeered the efforts of the hapless soldiers in the boats. The soldiers were then ordered out of the boats to try to free them from the mud.

From his vantage point on the wagon seat, Muddy cringed as he watched the soldiers flounder about and sink to their armpits in the soft mud. He didn't feel like laughing. How well he remembered his own terrifying experiences along the same shore. Except for being scared, he had made it to shore without too much trouble. But he realized these men, fully-clothed in battle uniforms and

weighted down with rifles and ammunition, had no chance of reaching shore in battle-ready condition.

"Don't waste your ammunition," ordered Lieutenant Dowling. "We'll get to them later," he promised. "They'll not be going anywhere." Again Muddy was humiliated by his side.

"Here comes the *Uncle Ben!*" shouted Jo Bear. He waved his hands, pointing to the north toward Sabine Lake. Even Muddy knew the cotton-clad steamer would be no match for any of the gunboats. Compared to the sleek warships, she resembled a dirty, fat duck, belching smoke as she slowly moved toward Sabine City. He knew two or more layers of cotton bales tied to her deck hid twelve-pounders. Bales of cotton would also protect her boilers. This ridiculous-looking vessel, along with the *Josiah Bell,* comprised part of General Magruder's so-called fleet. Muddy had seen one of them docked at Beaumont. Most of the time the steamers stayed in the upper reaches of Sabine Lake, near the Neches and Sabine rivers, guarding the approaches to Beaumont and Orange. When Jo Bear decided the *Uncle Ben* was going to stand out in the lake, he urged Muddy to leave their vantage point and mingle with the crowd.

"Come on, Muddy. The *Uncle Ben*, she's gonna wait and catch any Yanks the Guards miss. Me, I think she's gonna have herself a mighty long wait." Even though he didn't share his sentiment, Muddy obliged his friend and followed him down into the crowd. They walked about, picking up what news they could as they edged up to groups of adults. Someone called out the latest action.

"The couriers are back!" The boys turned and saw the white cloud of dust trailing the horses coming down the shell road from Taylor's Bayou. The riders waved their broad-brimmed hats at the crowd waiting for their report.

"I guess them couriers got the word out," was Jo Bear's smug remark to his silent friend. But Muddy refused to take the bait. He had learned to be cautious in predicting what either side was doing or planning.

By three o'clock in the afternoon, the crowd had lost most of its enthusiasm. There had been no more firing from the Union ships.

Muddy and Jo Bear were lying on the embankment as they waited for some activity. Then Muddy sat up and brushed the grass from his hands with sharp, decisive movements. He was mentally washing his hands of the whole Yankee fleet. It had taken him an hour of hard thinking while Jo Bear dozed beside him. "Ain't gonna be no battle, Jo Bear. Now, it's up to me." Muddy's grief-stricken voice seemed to alert his buddy.

"Now, hold on. You ain't planning—"

"Yes. Right now. It's time. Miz Banks won't miss me until chore time." He turned to push himself to a standing position.

Jo Bear grabbed him by the waistband and jerked him back to the grassy incline. "You ain't going nowhere. You belong here with Miz Banks."

Muddy shoved his friend and moved to get up again. "Not anymore. I ain't ever gonna be freed—not by them Yankees. I got to do it myself." Both boys were on their feet. Jo Bear had Muddy's arm in both fists. "Let go. It's something I've got to do," pleaded Muddy. "I promised my mammy." He knew the scrappy Cajun might create a scene and block his plan. Jo Bear hung on, not saying a word, just shaking his head back and forth. Muddy gave a mighty jerk on his arm and broke free. But it wasn't enough. The Cajun boy dived for his legs. Both boys rolled down the embankment.

"I ain't gonna let you up until you say you ain't gonna go, Muddy Banks." Jo Bear now had both arms wrapped around one of Muddy's legs as he sat on Muddy's backside.

Muddy twisted and squirmed but couldn't throw Jo Bear off. He reached up and grabbed a handful of Jo Bear's hair, giving a vicious yank. Jo Bear let go with a wild yelp. Both boys were then on their knees facing each other. This was their first real fight.

Muddy was the first to speak. "You lied. You promised in blood not to tell, Jo Bear Prejean."

"But Muddy—"

"But nothing!"

"Maybe the Yanks will come back," was Jo Bear's desperate suggestion.

"Sure, sure they will. A hundred years from now."

"What about Miz Banks? What if'n they do come back. Don't you care what those men might do to Miz Banks? They might—" Jo Bear's imagination left him speechless at that prospect.

Thoughts of escaping to freedom drained from Muddy as he listened to Jo Bear's unspoken supposition. He turned and buried his face in his arms in the soft grass and began to sob. "Oh, Jo Bear, why'd you have to say that? She saved my life. Now I know I can't leave. Not unless I know Miz Banks will be safe." Jo Bear dropped to his knees beside his friend. His face was working as he tried not to weep for his buddy.

"Please, Muddy. It's gonna get better. Honest. Maybe you can go shrimping one time with Captain Placette and me. And maybe we'll build us a sailboat." In an effort to cheer him, he was reminding Muddy of their previous dreams and plans.

"I know. And maybe when I grow some more, Miz Banks'll sell me."

"Ain't so, Muddy Banks! How can you say that?"

Muddy got to his feet, wiped his face on his sleeve, and stared at his friend for a long moment. "If you were a slave, you'd understand about buying and selling." His gaze swept over the marshlands southward, over the route he had planned to take. His shoulders sagged for a moment, then straightened. There was no way he could make Jo Bear understand his need to be free. He turned to his now silent friend. "I guess I'm done thinking about running away for now. My place is with my family, and that's Miz Banks."

Jo Bear gave a deep sigh, then lunged at Muddy, throwing him to the ground. He sat astride the surprised boy and began yelling in a jubilant voice. "Muddy, you black son-of-a-gun, you done scared me half silly!" Muddy began struggling to free himself, but he was smiling. He was glad his goodbye to Jo Bear and Miz Banks had been postponed.

Before the boys could unscramble themselves, Mrs. Dorman rode up beside them in her carriage.

She sat there, sternly eyeing the embarrassed boys who were struggling to their feet. Then she said, "Muddy, Miz Banks wants you at the house at once. She needs you." She quickly wheeled her team about and rushed off.

Chapter 17

"YOU COMING, TOO, JO BEAR?"

"Naw. Miz Banks told me I don't have to go back until the firing starts." Muddy knew it was useless to argue. He ran home, wondering why Miz Banks was at the house and not at the doctor's office, or at the newly set up field hospital with Captain Bailey, the army doctor. He knew it was time she had finished her baking.

Surprised at seeing the breadcart from the hotel pulled up at the back porch, he called out, "Miz Banks, how come—"

She appeared at the door and did not let him finish his question. "I'm glad you got here so fast. Wash up. I need you to run an errand for me." He washed, still curious. She came out on the porch as he was drying his hands. "I've some sweet rolls on the table. I want you to take them to the Command Post. Captain Odlum needs—"

This time he interrupted her. Resentment filled his voice. "You promised I wouldn't have to help the enemy. Now you want me to take them something to eat." He said it fast before he lost his courage. "No, Miz Banks, that's helping, and I don't have to do it. You said so." She stopped in her rush about the kitchen collecting supplies and whirled about to face the adamant black boy.

"I know I promised you wouldn't have to help your enemies. But this is food, not guns or bullets. I'm not asking you to engage in warfare. I'm asking you to help me get food to some hungry men."

"If they ain't fed, they'll be too weak to fight is the way I see it." Never before had he talked back or openly defied her. She had to understand. And it seemed she did. The shocked look on her face softened to one of sympathy.

"Muddy, I don't like this war. I know you expect to be made free if we're defeated. But I don't think you understand what I'm asking and my reasons for asking." She carefully wiped her hands on her apron. Her brow wrinkled in deep thought. He kept still. What was she planning to do to him? He watched her chew at her bottom lip for a moment. But her hand was gentle when she placed it on his shoulder and spoke.

"You must understand what I asked you to do is not asking you to be disloyal. Now it seems I must do something sooner than I planned. Let's go into the parlor." He followed her, mystified. Was she going to sell him to someone else? He wasn't crippled, but since he had grown so much, maybe she did not want him around anymore. He had heard some people would pay a thousand dollars for slaves his size. Maybe he should change his mind and help her before she did something awful, like sell him.

She must have read the fear in his face. Before he could say anything, she grabbed his shoulder. He stiffened instinctively. Did she think he would run away again? She must have, for he heard her say, "Don't run, Muddy. Your running days are over. Trust me." He relaxed. The knot in his stomach disappeared. This was the same woman who had taken him in and treated him so kindly. She was his family.

He had seldom been in the parlor. The heavy, carved furniture and the draperies at the closed windows gave off musty odors from being closed up in the damp climate of the Gulf Coast. He watched her take a small key from its hiding place in the vase on the mantle. With it, she opened a drawer in the tall secretary. He moved closer to watch her take out a large, brown envelope. She turned and faced him.

"Sit down over there on the sofa. I have something to give you." Puzzled, he dusted the back of his britches before sitting down on the damask-covered couch. Then she began. "You know I've never held to the idea of owning slaves. We've talked about it. Remember?" He nodded. "But I had to buy you to save your life and keep you off Boss Jordan's boat. Right?" Again he nodded. What did that have to do with his refusing to take the rolls to Captain Odlum's office? Before he could voice that question, she continued.

"Do you remember that day I went to Beaumont soon after your experiences with the rolls and preparing the fryers for Lieutenant Dowling?"

He grinned as he recalled that day. He had finally begun to like fried chicken again. She waved the papers she held in front of his perplexed face. "I went to Beaumont, to the courthouse, to have these papers drawn up." She moved to sit across from him in one of the large leather-upholstered chairs as she spoke. "First, I want you to see the Bill of Sale Boss Jordan gave me when I purchased you. Please read it aloud. I know this is the first time you've seen it, but I'll help you with the hard words." She handed the paper to him.

He took it and looked at it. His hands were trembling. This was proof he had been sold. It was just like the papers Lieutenant Dowling signed when he bought eggs and chickens from Miz Banks. Only, he noticed quickly, it had more writing and a purple seal stuck to it at the bottom. He began to read it aloud.

Tears rolled down his cheeks as he finished reading. He made no effort to wipe them away. *Me and the chickens,* he thought. *No difference.*

Bethel gently removed the Bill of Sale from his fingers. "Now, don't cry. Read this one, please." She handed him the other paper. It was heavier, and it crackled when he grasped it. Of course he would do what she asked. *He was her slave, wasn't he?* He did not say that out loud. Instead he began to read from the new paper.

BILL OF SALE

State of Texas ⎱
County of Jefferson ⎰

        Know all men by these presents, that for the sum of one dollar and other considerations, I, Bethel Banks, widow of Sid Banks, do hereby relinquish my right, title, and claim to said purchaser _____

[Muddy Boy Banks was penciled in the blank], a Negro slave named Boy—

"But that's my old name. That's me!"
"Yes, but read on, Muddy."

He is described as follows: Approximate age, twelve years old. Height: 5'5." Weight 130 lbs. Outstanding identifying markings being: medium color and scar on calf of right leg.

        In accepting this bill of sale for his own person, said purchaser agrees to become a Ward of Jefferson County Court until a suitable guardian is appointed.

        Signed:_____*Bethel Banks*_____
                               Owner

        Signed:_____
Witnessed by: Purchaser

_____

    Muddy sat very still. His eyes stared unseeing at the paper in his hand. He did not quite understand all he had read. He sensed something tremendous was taking place. He reread it silently, mouthing each word.

    Bethel spoke softly, as though she, too, recognized the importance of the occasion. "I wanted to ink in your new name, but I don't know it. When you choose, we'll put it on the paper, and let you sign it, too." He hardly heard what she was saying. The paper said he would have to buy himself. Money? He had no money. All the money he had earned had been spent on the pocketwatch and paying Jo Bear to help him with the fryers. When he realized this, he threw the paper to the floor and buried his face on the back of the sofa. Sobs racked his body.

"Why, Muddy. It's your freedom paper. This is what you've been wanting. I would've given it to you sooner, but I was waiting for you to decide on a name. Then we got so busy, I decided to give it to you for Christmas." She moved to his side and placed her arm around him. "Don't cry, Muddy. Tell me what's troubling you."

He jumped up, knocking her arm from his shoulder. "Oh, Miz Banks! Why do you trick me so? You know I don't have any money. And about the other considerations," he stuttered over the long word, "I don't even know what that is."

"Dear me, Muddy. It looks as though I got the cart before the horse. Yes, you do have some money." She smiled as she reached into the large envelope once more and pulled from it a smaller envelope and handed it to him. The envelope was not flat and smooth, but lumpy and weighed a lot for its size. When he looked into the envelope, his eyes grew big and disbelief swept across his face. Dropping to his knees, he dumped the contents of the envelope on the soft carpet in front of him.

"Miz Banks! This is my money? United States money?" Instinctively, he bit into one of the coins. "How come you say this is my money?"

"Young man, I've told you time and time again I do not believe in slavery. So how could I work you and not pay you even that small amount?" She pointed to the pile of coins on the carpet. "That would have been treating you as a slave. I put money in that envelope each week from the day you began to do chores for me. I couldn't pay you much, but what with your keep and my teaching you a trade, it made me feel better about owning you."

"But that wasn't work you get paid for," he said. "It was chores. You told me."

"Yes, I told you that. I wanted you to feel a real part of my household. And you are. You never were a lazy boy. You deserved pay. It was to be a part of the Christmas surprise." She paused as he wiped his tears with his handkerchief. "Now, back to the business at hand." She stood erect, towering over him. "Muddy Boy Banks, do you wish to purchase one negro slave boy from me, Bethel Banks, a widow, for the sum of one dollar?"

He stood in front of her, a silver dollar clenched in his hand. "I do," he said solemnly, extending the coin to her. She took it, and dropped it into her apron pocket.

Muddy buys himself

"Well, that's settled, at last." But he pulled at her sleeve, stopping her from leaving the room.

"What about the rest I owe you."

"The rest?"

"That 'other considerations' part."

"Oh, Muddy, you have already paid me that part. Don't you know that? What 'other considerations' means in this sale is the many kind things you've done for me. It means the many times you did not fuss about having to work so hard. It means your willingness to learn the things I've taught you." Now she was crying, openly and unashamed, as she hugged the boy against her bony frame.

"I'm free? I'm really free, at last?"

"Yes. But being an orphan, or being without known parents, you've become a ward of the county."

"What does that mean?" Muddy dropped to the floor and huddled over his money. *Was this white folks double talk?* He was ashamed of that thought. He knew he could trust Miz Banks.

"Until you're of age, you have to be under the care of an adult or group of people for your own good. If you were to live by yourself, someone might steal you and sell you back into slavery. If you're sick or hurt, there'll be someone to look after you. Someone is needed to clothe you, and see that you learn to take care of yourself. That's what a guardian does. It's not the same as owning. Captain Placette is Jo Bear's guardian. Doctor Murray had the papers drawn up when Jo Bear came to live with the Captain. Jo Bear's free. You know that. So, if you're willing, the Court can appoint me as your guardian. You can continue to work and live here until you're old enough to attend to your own affairs." She looked down at him, for he was still silent, trying to comprehend what she was telling him. "Muddy, if anyone lays a hand on you, they'll have to answer to me. Understand?"

She let him think through all she had told him. He asked, "When I'm full grown, I can leave and go anywhere I please?"

"Yes. Yes, you can. And we'll discuss your schooling and your plans for the future just as I did with my own children."

"And no one can kick me or shove me around?"

"That's right. The court and I will be sworn to protect you." His chest swelled with pride. He was a real person at last. He clapped his hands and laughed out loud.

"Wait 'til old Jo Bear hears I'm free. You gonna whup up on him if'n he lays a hand on me, too?" he asked, slyly.

She laughed at his question. "Now I believe you can handle Jo Bear and his roughhousing."

Muddy flexed his muscles, and waved his arms high over his head in his excitement. "I have to go tell him."

Her face became serious once more. She placed both hands on his shoulders, forcing him to look up at her. He could tell what she was about to say was going to be very important to him. "I called you into the parlor to free you. This was necessary before I could explain why I think it is important for you to take the rolls to Captain Odlum's office. Remember?"

"Yes, Ma'am. But there's other slaves here. I'm still wanting them to be free."

"And you should. This has to do with another attitude you should have about all people. This is not just a war about slavery. It's about the sovereign right of a state to control its own affairs. I don't have time to explain that now. I'm not asking you to take up arms against the Federal troops. I'm talking about being kind and doing decent things when you can for all people. It's the same when I help

Doctor Murray or Doctor Bailey nurse any wounded soldier, no matter which side he has served. This has nothing to do with war. You may not believe as Captain Odlum and his Guards do, but you count them as friends. Haven't they spent time with you and Jo Bear explaining their work?" He nodded. "And Lieutenant Dowling? He thinks you're quite a worker. And Captain Placette? He's a Southerner who's gone for reinforcements. Would you give him food if he were hungry?"

"Miz Banks, this having a war is terrible, ain't it?"

"Yes, it is. But do you understand why we should be concerned with doing good when we can? And now you have the right to choose. So I'm asking again. Will you help me take food to the captain or to anyone needing food this day or any day?"

He bent his head and stopped to gather up the coins from the floor. After putting them in the envelope, he handed it to her for safekeeping before answering. "I think I understand. I'll do it. I know you wouldn't make me—ask me, to do anything wrong." He nodded his head emphatically. "I'll do it."

Chapter 18

MUDDY moved among the officers as he served the coffee and sweet rolls. Commodore Leon Smith and Captain W. S. Good had arrived on horseback from Beaumont. The couriers sent by Captain Odlum had reached them in time. He wondered if the courier sent to General Magruder had reached him. He listened as he served the men. He wished Jo Bear could be there and hear, too. All the men seemed to think the small fort had little or no chance for survival. Muddy was glad but did not let his emotions betray him.

Captain Odlum was urging the men to go and inspect the fort. After they left the office, Muddy gathered up the dishes and stacked them in the cart outside. He tried to be careful as he pushed the cart to the kitchen door of the hotel, as Miz Banks had instructed him. She had promised him that once the cart and its contents were delivered to the hotel, he would be free to return to the fort.

It was not long before Muddy joined Jo Bear on the seat of the ammunition wagon parked on the western fringe of the fort. "What's happening, Jo Bear? Have you heard anything?"

"Naw. Those Yanks are scared. Around noon it looked like the warships were coming up the channel. Don't know what happened, unless the transports got in the way."

"Maybe they're waiting for some more ships." Muddy was determined he was not going to crawfish around the jubilant Jo Bear. He hugged the knowledge of the officers' meeting and their opinions to himself. "Look! They're coming!" He stood up in his excitement as he spotted the Union ships beginning to move up the six-mile channel.

"More ships?" hooted Jo Bear. "Those Yankees have done raised the water level so high with all those ships I 'spect the beaches will be flooded any minute now." His laughter rang out over the heads of the people below.

"You shut up that smart talking or I'm gonna push you off this wagon," was all Muddy said. Before Jo Bear could react, a roar from the spectators grabbed their attention.

"Here they come! Here they come! Take cover! Take cover!" Lieutentant Dowling shouted from the top of one of the covered bombproofs.

"We'd better go, Jo Bear."

"No, wait. They ain't begun no fighting, yet."

"But Doctor Murray said—"

"I know, I know. Just wait. We got plenty time."

The Yankee warships, the *Sachem* and the *Arizona,* veered up the Louisiana channel side. Jo Bear slapped Muddy on the back. "You see that? They're gonna try that side. Man, they're gonna be up to their decks in mud." True to his prediction, the two ships' forward progress halted abruptly. They were stuck fast in the mud.

Captain Odlum, who had been running back and forth between the fort and command headquarters in Sabine City, called to Lieutenant Dowling. "Shoot at the wheelhouses. They won't be going anywhere with their wheel ropes severed." The boys watched and listened as Captain Odlum and two of his captains made preparations to go for reinforcements. Doctor Murray joined the men and spoke briefly with them.

Before leaving the fort area, Doctor Murray rode up to the wagon and yelled "Git!" at Muddy and Jo Bear. The boys fell to the ground in their haste to obey. Choking on the dust of the riders, they ran back to the house.

As the cannon from the *Sachem* roared its assault, Muddy pulled at Jo Bear, urging him on. But the shells fell short of the fort. The boys ran through the house and up the stairs to the widow's walk. Muddy's watch showed ten to four. Miz Banks must be with Doctor Bailey, he decided, since the house was empty.

Jo Bear began screaming, "Tell them to fire, Lieutenant!" But the guns at the fort were quiet. The boys watched the Commodore dash out and wave a Confederate flag. Then he joined the riders going for reinforcements. This left Lieutenant Dowling in command. Puffs of smoke from the Parrott guns on the deck of the *Arizona* were plainly visible to the boys.

"You see that?" Muddy pointed toward the *Arizona*.

"Yes. But she's floundering. That old mud is grabbing her sides. Look at the Guards! They're getting ready! The *Sachem* is free and coming up!"

"Are they abreast of the poles yet?"

"Now!" The first cannon from the fort fired. "Over-shot! Lieutenant Dowling gonna peel their heads."

"Boom!" rang the second cannon from the fort.

"They missed!" Muddy didn't gloat. He wanted to laugh and to cry at the same time. How could he support both sides? He wanted the South to lose, but not here. "They missed again, Jo Bear." The third and fourth shots also missed. Jo Bear looked disgusted but said nothing. Then a roar of delight from the soldiers and townspeople followed the fifth shot. Michael McKernan and his twenty-four-pounder had scored a direct hit through the hull of the *Sachem*. Jo Bear jumped up and down, screaming all the while. The other five cannon of the fort found range, and each struck wood and metal. The sixth howitzer, after firing the sixth shot, backed off its platform, rendering it useless. An obliging current swung the damaged *Sachem* into the mudbank, and there it was, locked bow and stern across the channel.

"They got the *Arizona*'s mast!"

Before Muddy could think up a proper retort, McKernan put a shot through the *Sachem*'s steam drum. Scalding water poured out on the helpless men on her decks. Screams of pain echoed over the water. Many sailors and riflemen jumped overboard. The boys were quiet. For the first time they seemed to understand men would be killed and wounded before the battle ended.

Jo Bear muttered, "I didn't want nobody hurt, Muddy."

"I know that. But that's what happens in war. Oh, Jo Bear, here comes the *Clifton* up the Texas channel." They watched as the

Clifton's guns hurled broadsides into the southfacing bastion of the the fort. The *Clifton* moved majestically up the channel, firing steadily. The Guards gave answering fire. The men at the fort could be seen digging out one of the twenty-four pounders, lowering the cannon.

"They got to get it down," explained Jo Bear. "It's overshooting." Then a shout went up. With the first barrage, a shot from the fort hit the *Clifton*'s wheelhouse. The helmsman, his guidelines severed, watched helplessly as the ship grounded. Another shot hit the *Clifton*'s boiler. Fire broke out on the damaged ship. Sharpshooters aboard who were not burned began to shoot at the exposed gunners at the fort.

Muddy and Jo Bear were silent. Smoke from the fort's cannon lay in the haze around the heads and shoulders of the Guards. Time and again the men at the fort exposed themselves, trying to see. The *Arizona,* grounded at the stern in the mud, lowered small boats to pick up survivors from the *Sachem* and the *Clifton.*

"Look over there in the marshes!" Jo Bear pointed to the Louisiana side. A group of ragged men in coonskin caps had risen from the rushes and were firing their muskets and rifles. "Them's Cajuns, just like me. Trappers, them." Jo Bear was jumping up and down, shouting as though the men might be able to hear him. In his excitement, his foot slipped on the tin surface of the walk and he slid between the railings and the rooftop. Muddy grabbed him just in time to keep him from plunging down the sloping roof.

"You crazy Cajun! I told you to be still." He pulled the chastened boy back to safety.

"Where'd they go, Muddy?" They searched the marshes for the riflemen, but they were gone.

"Are they dead?"

"Naw, Muddy. They're playing hide-and-seek with the Yanks." But he didn't say it with much confidence. They continued to watch the exchange of shots. The blue haze of smoke finally obscured their view of the fort. The acrid smell of gunpowder wafted inland on the Gulf breeze.

"Look, Muddy! They're striking their colors."

"What does that mean?"

"There, look at the *Clifton*. See, they've hauled down their colors and are raising the white flag. And so is the *Sachem*. That means they're giving up!"

"Look, Jo Bear! The *Arizona* is doing it, too! What does it mean? What happens now?"

"Mean? It means they've surrendered! It means we've won, Muddy!" Jo Bear collapsed on the tin roof and began to bang on the floor with both fists.

"Not me. I ain't surrendered. Anyway, it's too soon. The battle can't be over. It's only four-thirty." He dangled his watch in front of Jo Bear's face. "Whoever heard of a battle lasting only forty-five minutes?"

"You have. I have. Now, the whole United States of America will hear tell of it. Wheeee!" he yelled at the top of his lungs.

"Hang on, there. I ain't gonna pull you back again."

"I'm hanging. I'm hanging. Look, there goes that red-headed Irishman."

"Where?" The haze was lifting and moving inland, away from the fort. Muddy brushed the tears from his eyes and stared as Jo Bear pointed.

"Over there. That man with the white flag tied to his saber. That's the lieutenant."

"Where's he going?"

"He's got to let them Yankees surrender."

"I ain't gonna watch no more."

"Aw, Muddy, don't be mad. Now there won't be killing anymore. Aren't you glad about that?"

"I don't know. Hey, look!" He pointed, wheeling the other boy around toward the channel.

"Aw, me. The *Arizona* is getting away. And that other ship that was coming up the channel is turning, too."

"But, Jo Bear, you said she surrendered. How come she's getting away?"

"Who's to stop her? 'Pears like to me Lieutenant Dowling done got a bear by the tail. He can't chase her. And who's gonna guard all them men with their hands in the air wading out of the water? And all those men on the *Clifton* and the *Sachem*? And those men back at the old fort?" His questions went unanswered. The boys remained on the roof to watch the more than six hundred prisoners surrender to a surprised, shirtless, powder-stained Lieutenant Dick Dowling of Company F of Colonel Joseph J. Cook's First Texas Heavy Artillery Regiment.

Chapter 19

MUDDY slowly pushed the breadcart through the rows of pallets in the makeshift field hospital set up near the fort. The low moans of the more seriously burned soldiers and sailors mingled with the murmur of voices from the small clusters of prisoners sitting around the campfires outside the main tent. Muddy tried to avert his eyes as he passed the wounded. This is terrible, he thought. But he was glad to help. One of Dowling's men had brought word from Miz Banks, and a list of supplies she needed to help Doctor Bailey at the hospital. He was glad he might help ease the pain of the wounded.

Jo Bear had gone with Captain Placette earlier to cull the channel for any useable staples left afloat. The fleeing battleship *Arizona* and the transport ships had thrown their supplies overboard, even horses and mules, to lighten their vessels in order to cross the bar and escape. It was dark now, but before he had delivered the supplies, Muddy had stood on the widow's walk watching the lights of the small vessels running up and down the channel gathering salvage.

Little order prevailed in Sabine City. The citizens and the Guards were celebrating the victory. Lieutenant Dowling was hard put to keep the Guards in line and see that the many able-bodied prisoners did not escape. Wagonloads of spectators had come from as far as Beaumont. What a mess! Muddy tried to picture what it would have been like if the Yanks had won. But that picture of victory eluded him, for all he could see in his mind's eye was a devastated Sabine City with all his friends killed.

Bethel spotted Muddy and hurried to his side. Quickly she checked the contents of the cart. Fatigue was etched in every line of her long face. "Thank you," she said. "Now, follow me," she ordered, as she pulled her rolled-up sleeves down and buttoned the cuffs at her wrists. They stopped by the first pallet inside the tent. The soldier was unconscious.

Muddy waited patiently as she tried to talk to the next prisoner. He handed her the cup of milk and watched as she held it for the wounded man to drink. His hands were bandaged with torn sheets from the hotel. Like the other scalded prisoners, he was covered with flour from head to toe. Doctor Bailey and his helpers had lost no time in using the recovered barrels of flour thrown overboard by the escaping Yankee fleet.

As they moved down the line giving food and drink to the wounded, Muddy noticed a tall Yankee sea captain watching Miz Banks. He stood behind some stacked crates he was using as a makeshift desk. When they reached his side, he bowed from the waist and addressed Miz Banks.

"A down-Eastern voice if I ever heard one. Your servant, Madam. Frederick Crocker, master of the captured sidewheeler steamer, the U.S.S. *Clifton*." His voice dripped bitterness, even as he added in a lighter tone, "and lately of New Bedford."

Bethel smiled as she dropped into a deep curtsy. "Bethel Crenshaw Banks, daughter of Eb Crenshaw of the whaler *Henry Pike* out of Portland." She straightened and added in a much softer voice, "Now known as the Widow Banks of Sabine City, Texas."

A small smile hovered around the tight-lipped sailor. "You may be a Texan now, but there's no denying the jib of your sail or the sound of your voice." He motioned for her to sit down on a nearby empty flour keg. Muddy moved back out of the way but stood close enough to hear the two displaced New Englanders talk. And listening wasn't easy for him. She and the captain talked so fast it made his head ache to listen. About every other word came through for him. Miz Banks was telling the captain about the war and how she hated it.

"Pitting brother against brother," she said. "This war is doing nothing but tearing our nation apart."

The captain seemed inconsolable over the loss of his ship and the injuries to his crew. "There is no excuse for such a performance as we gave this day. Our intelligence reports must have been gathered by numbskulls. I rue the day the idiot idea of serving my country caused me to take leave of my senses and offer my services." He smacked the crates with his fist, nearly toppling them. "Madam, do you realize the magnitude of what took place today?" He began to pace back and forth. "I never witnessed such bungling and incompetence in my life. Even the youngest apprentice seaman on my whaler could have handled this affair better."

His face was red with chagrin. "Imagine the embarrassment I suffered when young Dowling presented himself to accept my surrender. There he stood, shirtless, grease-smeared, smoke-stained, with a dirty white rag tied to his saber. I thought him to be a raw recruit. Instead, I find him in charge of the mighty forces—forty-three men!"

He stopped speaking and pulled up another keg and sat down. He wiped his brow with his handkerchief. Bethel merely patted his arm and kept quiet. Muddy burned with shame for the man. Captain Crocker cleared his throat, blew his nose, and then spoke again. The angry tone was gone from his voice. "How do you stand this heat? Already there is frost on the ground at home."

She laughed, seemingly relieved he had changed the subject. Muddy was glad, too. He wanted to hear no more about the mistakes of the North's navy, wherever it was.

Bethel poured the captain a cup of milk. Muddy handed him some cookies. Then she spoke. "Captain, these days will pass. Let us pray this war'll soon be over, and you'll soon be back on your ship." Then she turned to Muddy. She took him by the hand and presented him to Captain Crocker. "Captain, I want you to know my friend, Muddy Boy Banks."

Startled by the introduction, Muddy blurted out, "And, I'm free, sir. Miz Banks done set me free."

Captain Crocker patted Muddy on the shoulder. He then turned questioning eyes toward the widow. "You own slaves?" His voice was not so friendly, thought Muddy. Had he said something wrong?

"No, I don't," she answered. "But I did buy him." The captain listened as she told Muddy's story.

Finally he asked Muddy, "Can you read and write?"

"I'm learning."

"Good. You ought to learn a trade, too. No good in being free if you can't be independent."

"He can almost bake as well as I can. He's a hard worker and a quick learner," bragged his tutor. Muddy hung his head, embarrassed but delighted to hear her compliments. He didn't want the white people to see how proud he was of her praise.

"Well, Muddy Boy Banks, when you are full grown and have a name for yourself, come to Massachusetts. Any ship's captain would give you a job as ship's baker and pay you well." When the captain had said this, Bethel stood up and shook the loose flour from her skirts.

"Come on, Muddy. We must finish our rounds. Then you will have to go home and feed the stock. A battle doesn't mean a thing to a bunch of fractious laying hens and greedy turkeys."

Chapter 20

THE NEXT MORNING Jo Bear and Muddy stood
on the widow's walk, staring out over Sabine City and the Gulf. The
early morning sun created sparkles on the surface of the channel. A
cool, fall breeze blew in from the Gulf of Mexico, raising small
ripples in the smooth waters. The tide was in. The pre-dawn fog
had dissipated, leaving the green grass below moist and glistening.

"They're all gone, Muddy. Every yellow-bellied one of 'em," Jo
Bear bragged. "'Cepting of course, that old blockader, *Cayuga,* out
there bird-dogging the Pass."

"Yes," Muddy agreed, his voice low and ashamed. "They're
gone." How could just one day make all this difference? When he
saw the fleet of ships steaming up the channel the day before, he
had thought it would not be long until the Yankees were in control
of Sabine City and the fort. And maybe all of Texas. Instead, he
and Jo Bear had seen the Davis Guards capture prisoners and two
warships and send the rest of the invading ships back to sea.

Then he remembered the good thing that had happened that
same day. He was free! Miz Banks had given him his freedom
papers. Had Muddy known all negroes in Texas would be declared
free on the 19th of June, 1865, his unhappiness for the rest of his race
would not have been so keen.

Jo Bear was not noticing his quiet friend. He was still rejoicing.
"Boy, that was some battle, wasn't it? Now we got two more ships
for the Texas Navy." He shook Muddy's shoulder. "See, the *Uncle
Ben* done towed the *Sachem* over, and maybe we can salvage the
Clifton. Come on, let's go look at the prisoners. Maybe you and me
can get to talk to Captain Crocker." He urged Muddy down the
steps.

"Sh! Be quiet, Jo Bear. We don't want to wake Miz Banks. She
stayed up all night helping the doctors treat the wounded men."
Subdued, the pair tiptoed into the kitchen. Gone was the usual

heady odor of baking bread. The oven fires were banked. "See, she didn't bake the rolls. It's the first time since I came that's happened." Muddy walked over and peered into the fireboxes. "Jo Bear, me and you could bake for her. I could set the dough to rising. You could come back and help me make the rolls." He turned to his buddy for his answer.

Jo Bear seemed to study the offer for a few moments. "I kinda wanted to see the prisoners."

"You can go first and then come back by nine o'clock. I'll fix your breakfast and have it ready by then. I'll even let you carry my watch so you'll know when it's time to come back." Muddy cut his eyes toward his ever-hungry friend. Jo Bear loved that watch.

The combination of the hot breakfast and use of the watch got results. "All right. I'll be back. Now, gimme that watch."

Muddy handed him the watch with the warning, "Not one scratch, do you understand?"

True to his word, Jo Bear returned from his inspection of the prisoners at nine o'clock. Once more Muddy demanded Jo Bear scrub with soap. "Ah, but no," he pleaded when Muddy handed him the big apron. Muddy paid him no attention when he complained of the indignity of having to wear it. He pulled the sash tighter under Jo Bear's armpits. This time, Muddy explained, they would have to do a better job of kneading. As they worked, they talked quietly.

"Did you see Captain Crocker?"

"No. He wasn't there. They said he was at Captain Odlum's office making out his report. The Yanks sent one of their ships in under a white flag to ask about the prisoners." Leave it to Jo Bear, thought Muddy. He'd find out exactly what was happening. But he was glad his buddy hadn't seen the captain. He was afraid the man might prefer talking with the French boy.

Jo Bear was busy filling the last tray. "Won't Miz Kate be surprised when she finds out we made the rolls?" said Muddy.

"Won't Miz Banks be surprised when she see this mess we done made?" Both boys began to laugh. "You is white as me," giggled Jo Bear, pointing to the flour-covered negro boy.

"And you look awful, you crazy Cajun."

Jo Bear picked up a handful of flour and swirled it toward Muddy, who was threatening him with the rolling pin. "Now, quit that, Jo Bear. We'll have a hard enough time cleaning this kitchen without you making it worser."

"I ain't gonna help you. You ain't said nothing about cleaning, just baking."

"But you will go get the bread cart, won't you?" pleaded Muddy.

"If'n I can have a roll and some preserves when I get back."

"Ain't you ever full? You just ate your breakfast."

"All right. Go get the cart yourself." Jo Bear nonchalantly pulled off the apron and gave it a big shake. Flour flew everywhere. He then ran out into the backyard with Muddy sneezing and chasing him.

"You come back here. You ain't gonna do me that way." He lunged for Jo Bear and both boys fell to the ground, rolling over and over on the grassy surface.

"Oh, yi yi!" howled Joe Bear, twisting and squirming under the weight of the larger boy. "Help me, somebody! A live ghost is holding me down." Muddy couldn't help laughing at his friend. He finally succeeded in pinning Jo Bear's shoulders to the ground.

"Give up?"

"No!" Then, "Yes, you hurting me," he whined.

"You ain't hurt. So shut up. You promise to go get the cart?"

"I promise. Now get off'n my middle. You have them rolls buttered and preserves handy when I get back." Muddy backed off, watching Jo Bear's every movement. He had learned the hard way not to trust him in a tussle. Jo Bear knew all the tricks of dirty fighting. But today Jo Bear was in a happy mood. Hadn't his side beaten the Yanks?

Chapter 21

"HE'S COMING! See the dust! Come quick, Muddy."
Jo Bear stuck his tousled head through the back door of the kitchen.
Muddy turned to Bethel, his face aglow, his eyes pleading.

"All right, Muddy. You can go for a little while. But mind you,
not over thirty minutes. We've baking to do this morning. There'll
be all those people coming from Houston and Galveston." He
placed the dish and towel on the table. Wiping his hands across the
seat of his trousers, he left the kitchen.

"Yes'm, Miz Banks," he called over his shoulder. "I'll be right
back." The boys raced to the side of the road in time to see Captain
Odlum and his aides ride past the house.

"I know a general's coming today, Muddy. Who do you think is
coming with him?"

"How do I know? It's only been three days since the battle.
Don't 'spect many people know about the celebration." The boys
continued to discuss the formal ceremony planned to honor the
Jefferson Davis Guards. Prince John, as most of the townspeople
called General Magruder, would conduct the services. Bethel had
explained it all to Muddy and Jo Bear the night before. Muddy
could not help but admire the popular leader. Doctor Bailey described the general as a "soldier's soldier." The Texas troops loved
him.

The boys watched as the visiting troops rode into town. "You
coming?" Jo Bear pulled at his friend's sleeve.

"No, I have to go back and help Miz Banks." He knew she had
said he could stay longer, but he turned and left his surprised
buddy. He ran, for he did not want Jo Bear to see his tears of frus-
tration. He wanted no part of the victory celebration. He hid in
the barn while he tried to think. Then he decided it was no use. He
would have to talk to Miz Banks. She'd know.

"You're back mighty soon."

"I didn't want to watch any more. Miz Banks, what's gonna happen to Captain Crocker? Really happen to him?"

"I don't know. Doctor Bailey told you yesterday the prisoners were being sent to Houston. I don't know where they will be sent from there."

"Will they treat him kindly?"

"I hope so." She began to cut the lard into the flour as she spoke. "Stir those peaches. I don't want them sticking to the pan."

"But you know different, don't you," he persisted.

"Muddy," she paused to stare at him, "all prison camps aren't bad. We can only trust these men will get good care."

"He might die, mightn't he? Captain Crocker is as good as dead already, ain't he?" Muddy's voice cracked and he beat the wall with his fist.

"No. No. No, he's not. He's not even wounded. He's an officer. He'll more than likely receive better treatment than most." She continued to work the pie dough as though normal activity would dispel his apprehension.

He was not comforted. He was back at the pot of peaches clanging the metal spoon against the pan as though attacking the Southern army. "Don't they care? They won the battle. What do they care about Yankee prisoners?"

"Now, Muddy," her tone was soft but firm. "Calm down. He's in God's hands. We all are. The South's bound to lose. Before this war is over, we might all see the inside of prison camps. But," she added at the sight of his terror-stricken face, "we won't cross that bridge until we come to it, will we?" She dusted her hands and placed her arms about his shoulders. "We don't have time to sit and grieve, do we? There's chores to be done—"

He clutched at her sleeve. "Could we help him escape?" His eyes pleaded as his face flushed at the audacity of his request. "Please, Miz Banks?"

"Of course not! He's a prisoner! You don't know what you're asking!"

"You did it for me," he pleaded.

"I bought you legally. I can't do that for Captain Crocker. I would be breaking the law. I did it to save your life. I might have to go to jail or be shot for being a traitor!"

"Shoot a woman?" His face blanched. "No, they don't do that, do they?"

"They would be within their rights, and they might." She handed him the rolling pin and indicated the mound of dough. "This is our work, and we'd best be about it." He took the pin and began mechanically to roll out the dough for the fruit pies as ideas for helping the captain escape swirled about in his feverish mind. Several minutes passed before a shuddering sigh escaped his lips. There was no way he could sneak him out of the camp, and no place he could hide the captain without endangering Miz Banks.

She seemed to sense his acceptance of the situation. "In a couple of days, when things are back to normal, I'll begin to teach you how to make and decorate cakes. And Muddy, we'll start reading the newspaper together so we can keep up with the war."

He looked at her and forced a smile to his face. He knew she was trying to make him feel better. Perhaps he would in a day or two.

Once the pies were in the oven, she said, "Check our list. What's our next chore?"

"Feed the stock and get ready all those fryers Lieutenant Dowling ordered for the barbecue tomorrow." Then he grinned. "Wonder if we can rope Jo Bear into helping this time?" Both of them laughed as they continued their work. After a long silence, Bethel took the broom from Muddy's hand.

"Let's rest a bit. Sit on the steps outside while I get some cookies and milk." He walked to the steps and sat down. She handed him his cookies and milk and seated herself in the porch rocker. A look of distress settled on her face as she observed the silent boy. "Muddy, what are you thinking about?"

He wants to help
Yankee Captain escape

146

"I'm studying hard about something."

"Tell me what's bothering you."

"It's my name. My new name."

"Have you decided?"

"I think so." He hoped she would not laugh. He wondered if the captain would be angry.

"Well, what is it? I'm glad you have finally picked out a name. Hurry, tell me."

He moved to stand in front of her chair. She stopped rocking. Her face was as serious as his. "It's going to be Frederick Crocker Banks, if I'm permitted."

"Permitted? Why, Muddy—I mean Frederick, I think he'll be most pleased you've chosen his name."

"You don't think he'll mind having a black boy use his name?"

"I know he won't. We'll tell him ourselves."

"But they're sending him to Houston. You said so."

"I know, but we'll have time to visit him when I make my rounds with Doctor Bailey tonight."

"I can go, too?"

"Yes. Would you like to take Jo Bear with us? He's been wanting to meet Captain Crocker." She saw his frown. "You don't mind sharing your new friend with Jo Bear, do you?"

He had mixed emotions about sharing Captain Crocker with Jo Bear. Still, knowing Miz Banks would be disappointed in him if he said "No," he managed to grin.

"I'll tell Jo Bear to be ready after supper." She rose from the chair and headed for the kitchen. He put out his hand to stop her. "Miz Banks, 'fore we go back to work, would you show me how to write it? My new name?"

"Bring your copybook. But we must hurry." He did. She wrote in large, bold letters:

FREDERICK CROCKER BANKS

"Twenty-one letters, Miz Banks. That's a big name."

"A big name for a big young man. Now we have to start more pies." He placed the copybook up on a chair. Bethel smiled as she watched him stop and study the name each time he passed the chair. His lips moved silently as he learned the spelling of his new name.

Chapter 22

MUDDY laughed with Bethel as they followed the dancing Jo Bear down the road to the tent hospital. He envied the uninhibited white boy. How he'd like to shout the news from the widow's walk. "I'm free! I'm free! My name is Frederick Crocker Banks, and I'm free!" But instinct warned him to move cautiously in exercising his freedom after what Miz Banks had told him.

"Some people around here aren't ready for your news," she had said. "Prejudice is a terrible thing. Even the heroes of this battle are considered second-class citizens by many."

"The Irishmen? How can that be? They're white!"

"They are mostly ignorant, uncultured riffraff who live from day to day with no thoughts for the morrow. Some of them will better themselves, but most of them'll be content to live out their days roistering and eking out a living on the docks. It's all they know or care to learn."

"Why? Why is it so, Miz Banks?" He could not believe that of those hard-working men he had watched capture the *Clifton* and the *Sachem*.

"Some people are like that. That's why I'm so proud of you and your determination to better yourself. But you'll have to develop a thick skin. It isn't going to be easy for you." He saw tears in her eyes. He wondered how many people he knew would be glad to hear of his freedom. Doctor Murray would and Jo Bear, too.

Thinking of Jo Bear's reaction to his news brought his thoughts to the present. They were nearing the hospital tent. And his fear returned. Would Captain Crocker be pleased? He made certain his shirt was tucked in and his tie was straight. Miz Banks was dressed in her Sunday best, too. He tried to conceal his growing excitement. He didn't want Jo Bear to suspect.

Jo Bear dropped back beside Muddy and helped him pull the cart over the deep rut in the shell road. The cart was loaded with hot rolls and pastries for the prisoners. The cakes and pies bounced around but stayed in the cart. *Jo Bear is so quiet, he must be a little scared, too,* decided Muddy. It was the first time he had seen Jo Bear's unruly hair slicked down and combed. Old Jo Bear was in for a real surprise.

Bethel halted the boys outside the officers' quarters. "Wait here," she ordered. Muddy's pulse raced. He was alternately happy and scared. His stomach began to ache.

Jo Bear whispered, "What's she going to do? Why'd she go in there?" Muddy shook his head, unable to speak. He felt his face flush as the tall sea captain and Miz Banks came through the door of the tent. Jo Bear backed the cart, giving him a better view. Muddy could tell he was impressed by the size of the Yankee.

"Captain Crocker, Muddy's friend, Jo Bear Prejean, would like to meet you and shake your hand. Jo Bear, this is Captain Crocker." Muddy gave the awed boy a tiny shove toward the big man.

"Howdy, son. I hear you're a sailor like myself."

"Yes, sir," was all the usually talkative boy could answer.

Bethel spoke again. "Captain Crocker, I'd like for you to sign this document as a witness." Muddy's eyes widened in surprise. Document? He watched her reach into her satchel and pull out his freedom papers. "Muddy, will you read it out loud for the captain and Jo Bear?"

Him? Read in front of the captain and Jo Bear? Why was she doing this? But there she stood, holding the paper out to him. His first thought was to refuse. Surely she would understand. But being free was not going to make him a coward. He would read it. He would show them. He would not be ashamed if he made mistakes. Like she had always told him, all he could do was his best. He was glad he had read it over and over the night before.

He took the parchment and glanced over it, seeing that she had erased *Muddy Boy Banks* and substituted his real name. He began to read, not looking up at his audience of three.

". . . a negro slave named Frederick Crocker Banks being one and the same . . ." He continued reading the document until he had read it all. Jo Bear had sucked in his breath when he heard "Frederick Crocker Banks." The captain had made no sound.

Muddy raised his eyes to meet those of the woman who had befriended him. Her proud smile encouraged him. He turned to the captain. The man's face was stern as his eyes swept over Muddy's face and figure. Then he smiled and placed his hand on Muddy's shoulder.

"It's a good and honorable name you've chosen. You make me proud. I trust you will do nothing to besmirch it."

"No, sir. Thank you, sir." Muddy thought his heart would burst.

Jo Bear muttered "Whew!" in an evident sigh of relief. Bethel reached inside the satchel once more and pulled out her pen and a small bottle of ink. She turned and tipped over an empty box, placing the document on it.

"Would you be so kind as to witness this document?" The captain took the proffered pen and ink.

"I'd be honored, Madam."

"All right, Mudd—I mean Frederick. Will you please take the pen and sign your new name here?" She indicated the blank space. No one said anything as he laboriously wrote his name from memory. Then he handed the pen back to the captain, who in turn, let him hold the ink bottle while he signed in the proper place as a witness.

"There, now. It's all done and legal." Bethel rolled up the paper and placed it with the pen and ink back in the satchel. "When I asked Mudd—Frederick to make a peach pie, I didn't tell him why. Frederick," she said as she turned toward the cart, "in token of your appreciation for his time, and the privilege of bearing his name, please give Captain Crocker the pie you made all by yourself this afternoon."

He knew the exact location of that particular pie in the cart. He had been afraid she had intended it for General Magruder. How thankful he was he had done his best, in spite of thinking the Confederate general would get to eat it. He gravely presented the pie to the captain. It could have been the crown jewels of England from the way the captain bowed his acceptance.

"Thank you, Frederick. Wait here." He swung on his heel and entered the tent. He no longer held the pie when he returned. He held a slender case in his hand. "May I call you 'Freddy'? That was my name when I was your age." Muddy nodded and smiled. He tested it silently on his lips. The captain continued. "Miz Banks, I would like for you to have my spyglass as a token of my respect for you and for this occasion. I'd appreciate your leaving it to Freddy at your death."

"Why, Captain Crocker—"

"Please take it. I had it on my person when we had to surrender our ship. I'm certain I'll not be able to keep it, or need it for some time." His voice was sad, as if gauging his future. "In memory of this occasion, I'd like you to have these." They watched as he removed the insignia of his rank from his shoulders. He handed one to each boy.

"Thank you, sir. Thank you. I'll honor you and your name, sir." Tears of joy filled Muddy's eyes. Jo Bear mumbled his thanks, completely overcome by what he had seen.

Tears of gratitude and sadness mingled on Bethel's face as she clasped the captain's hand. "We shall pray for you each night. Thank you, Captain Crocker." He bowed low and shook the boys' hands before returning to his tent.

"Come on, boys," she sniffed. "Our work's just begun."

And Frederick Crocker Banks understood.

Epilogue

PERHAPS historians have neglected to record the Civil War battle of Sabine Pass, Texas, because it was so unbelievable. How could forty-one Irishmen, one cavalry surgeon, and a young engineer, behind crudely-built ramparts with only four thirty-two-pounders and two twenty-four-pounders accomplish all this in only one hour and forty minutes?

Capture two gunboats carrying fourteen guns,

Capture over six hundred prisoners,

Retrieve many rounds of ammunition plus a quantity of small arms,

Send three gunboats, seven transports carrying six thousand troops and a general back to sea,

Completely rout the remainder of an armada of twenty-seven ships,

And halt the long-planned invasion of Texas by Union forces for several months.

BUT THEY DID!

Suggested further reading:

Herbert and Virginia Gambrell. *A Pictorial History of Texas*. New York: E. P. Dutton, 1960.

Andrew Forest Muir. *Dick Dowling and the Battle of Sabine Pass*. Iowa State University publication, Vol. IV, No. 4, December 1958.

Frank X. Tolbert. *Dick Dowling at Sabine Pass*. New York: McGraw-Hill, 1962.

In addition, back files of *The Port Arthur* (Texas)*News* contain numerous stories on Sabine Pass, Port Arthur, and Dick Dowling.

Typesetting by *G & S, Austin*
Printing and Binding by *Edwards Brothers, Ann Arbor*
Design by *Whitehead & Whitehead, Austin*

The story takes place during the ___ War.
How does Muddy injur his leg?
Who does Bethel banks get to help her?
Who does Muddy keep refering to as his "rescuers"

What state does it take place in?

Bethel